PORTRAITS

Dancing

Through

Fire

KATHRYN LASKY

SCHOLASTIC INC.

New York Toronto London Auckland Sydney
Mexico City New Delhi Hong Kong Buenos Aires

To Meribah Grace Knight

Cover image:
Edgar Degas (1834–1917)
L'Étoile or *The Dancer on Stage*. Ca. 1876–1877
Pastel over monotype
Located in the Musée d'Orsay, Paris, France
Photography by Erich Lessing/Art Resource, New York

ISBN 0-439-71009-X

12 11 10 9 8 7 6 5 4 3 2 1   5 6 7 8 9 10/0

Printed in the U.S.A.
First printing, September 2005

PART ONE

PARIS 1870
Summer

Chapter 1

The small girl stood in just her underwear in front of the three grown-ups. It was cold for a June morning, and she tried not to shiver. She did not in any way want to do anything that might make her the least bit shorter than she already was. She wasn't sure if shivering did this, but she was trying her best to stand as straight as possible. Doctor Suchard pressed his cold fingertips against her spine, walking them up to the base of her neck, where one of her jet-black curls had escaped its comb. She felt the eyes of the two ballet mistresses scraping over her. She could hear them whispering to each other. Doctor Suchard said nothing. His silence was as bad as the women's whispers.

In the corner of the room, her mother sat, clutching the black umbrella. The hat on her head, with its sad pile of velvet roses, was wet and drooping from the rainy walk to the ballet school. The flowers looked as if they were suffering a slow, painful death and were about to drop their petals. Sylvie wished her mother hadn't worn that hat. She didn't much like it, and she felt it made them look as if they were trying too hard. Trying like Madame du Bac, the most meddlesome mother in the world. She was always pushing her two daughters in front of the teachers, always ambushing the *danseuses étoiles*, the stars, trying to flatter them. But, of course, if one was a *petit rat*, that was all life was about.

Yes, "little rats" was the name for these youngest pupils of the Paris Opera Ballet. And wasn't she, Sylvie herself, trying right now to somehow, miraculously, gain those three-quarters of an inch that teased and taunted and eluded her? For it was only three-quarters of an inch that stood between Sylvie Bertrand and advancement to the next level. She would then not be simply a little rat—a student—but a *true* member of the company. At four feet eleven and one-quarter inches, however, Sylvie was simply too short for even the *quadrille*, the lowest level of the five ranks of the Paris Opera Ballet.

The first part of the examination had been the easiest. This she felt she had done well. She saw the two ballet mistresses nodding as they watched her arm lifts, the *ports de bras*. The trick was that she must not appear as if she were *lifting* her arms but that they were simply, almost magically, floating up as effortlessly as a downy feather on a billow of wind. She was also turned out in her *tendus*, the leg extensions from which so much could be told about a dancer's abilities. And she had moved across the floor on a diagonal, stringing together elegant series of *pirouettes*. But now, when she had to stand perfectly still, she felt she had failed.

The doctor stopped pressing on her spine. He walked over to where the mesdames sat. Sylvie dared not look at the threesome, but she knew her mother's eyes were tracking them.

Then, one of the ballet mistresses, Madame Théodore, stood up. She adjusted the spectacles on her long, bony nose. She turned to Sylvie's mother.

"Madame Bertrand, although . . ."

Sylvie did not need to hear the rest. The word *although* told the entire story.

And now she must go to class and pretend as if nothing had happened. This would be the hardest part, especially since Madame Théodore herself was teaching the class.

"So?" Isabel, Sylvie's best friend, asked as Sylvie took her place at the *barre* in the rather dim and faded classroom. It was raining outside, and there was no sun to shine through the tall arched windows.

Tears brimmed in Sylvie's eyes. She shook her head and looked down. Isabel reached out and touched her shoulder. There was not much she could say. There were absolutely no comforting words for a dancer who failed to be advanced. Isabel herself had succeeded but was still required to take classes in the lower level.

"Three-quarters of an inch, Isabel. That is all I need."

"But, Sylvie, at least it is not like what happened with Marisol. She was tall enough but has no technique. She failed because she was sloppy. That would be worse."

"But she can improve," Sylvie said in a hoarse whisper.

"But you will grow, Sylvie."

"I hope so!" But her voice had not a trace of hope.

Madame Théodore entered the classroom. She tapped sharply on the floor with the tall stick that she carried to mark the counts. The violinist struck up the first chords of a Bach prelude. The rain continued to drum down on the windows until the panes appeared glazed with water and the room seemed to fill with shadows. Remnants of gilt and discolored marble yielded hints of a past grandeur.

The quiet opening notes of the Bach piece seemed almost suspended in the air as the young girls began their *barre* exercises. Suddenly, Sylvie noticed a man she had never seen before, sitting in the corner of the classroom. He was thin and had a neatly trimmed beard. His tall silk hat rested on the floor beside him, and he had a sketch pad on his lap. At his feet was a pile of discarded sheets from the pad.

Sylvie wondered who he was, and why he had been admitted to the classroom. The season subscribers were rarely permitted to observe class. Sylvie did not think she had ever seen one observing class as long as she had been dancing.

The tempo of the music increased. The exercises speeded up. Fifteen *tutus* lifted like puffy clouds as fifteen little rats began to unfold their legs in *grands développés*.

"Lift your chests! Lower your shoulders. Hips back!" Madame Théodore's shrill commands pierced the air. Every dancer at the *barre* lived in dread of being skewered by one of her barbed words. And could she put a sharp point on them! "Marisol, your arm looks like a dead fish," she snapped then.

Soon there was the break before center work. Sylvie wandered off into a corner with Isabel. She didn't feel like chatting with the other girls, especially Marie du Bac, who was exceedingly stuck-up. Sylvie noticed that the man in the corner had not stopped sketching. He was now regarding Stéphanie, who was sitting on the floor in a very ungraceful manner as she took off one toe shoe to adjust the cotton stuffing inside.

"Isabel, who is that man over there?" Sylvie asked.

"Monsieur Degas. They say that Marie du Bac has been posing for him, for a sculpture. As if she needed any more attention to puff her up!" Isabel cast a glance at Marie, who was *pirouette*-ing in front of the mirror, smiling at her image as she whirled by each time.

"Don't you hate the way she smiles at herself in the mirror? It's so fake," Isabel said.

"It looks painted on," Sylvie agreed.

Marie had a small, delicate head. She was undeniably pretty, with her flashing green eyes and coppery red hair. But Sylvie was most envious of Marie's feet; with their spectacularly high arch, they possessed the natural perfection that every ballerina longed for.

"Well, he's not drawing her now. He's drawing Stéphanie," Isabel pointed out.

"So he is." Sylvie wondered if the artist might ever draw *her*.

Madame Théodore rapped on the floor to signal that class was to resume.

Center work was normally Sylvie's favorite part of the class. It was also the most challenging. This was when the ballerinas were asked to attempt perfect balance and symmetry. But today, nothing felt right to Sylvie as she took a position between Isabel and Marisol (who was now so conscious of her arms that she was holding them straight out as if they were in casts).

Sylvie immediately sensed that her own center work would be disastrous. Nothing in her body felt aligned. Sylvie knew that everything in dance began not in one's legs but at the very core of one's body. That was the center of strength for a dancer, and now, with no *barre* for balance or support, this core was put to the test. But Sylvie felt something in her was slightly askew.

They began with the same exercises that they had done at the *barre*, but by the time they were asked to do an *arabesque*, Sylvie experienced a horrid sensation: Her legs felt like lead, her feet like pancakes, and every part of her seemed floppy and ugly. Madame Théodore walked by and stopped.

"Are you alive and pretending to be dead or dead and pretending to be alive, Sylvie?" she snapped. "You look like a corpse, not a dancer!"

"*Non*, madame," Sylvie whispered, and she felt some unnamable thing inside her shatter. She could almost hear it.

Class finally ended. Sylvie's mother was waiting for her on the steps of the opera house's back entrance.

"But Madame Théodore said you are very strong. That means, Sylvie, that they might make an exception in perhaps a month or two if you still have not grown."

Madame Bertrand and Sylvie moved through the narrow cobblestone street. As they turned the corner on the Rue le Peletier, away from the opera house, they hunched their shoulders and ducked their heads against the driving wind that had suddenly lashed out at them.

"Mama, not to the hole, please. I am not in the mood." Sylvie looked pleadingly at her mother. Her eyes, fringed by thick lashes, were very dark, with flecks of amber sparkle. Then a shadow appeared and extinguished the sparkles. She wrinkled her nose and pressed her plumpish lips into a rigid line of disapproval. A small dimple appeared on the left side of her chin. It was her frown dimple, as opposed to her smile dimple, which flashed in her cheek when she laughed.

"Don't speak nonsense — in this weather! But I heard they have made great progress. The foundations are almost complete. He is something, that Monsieur Garnier!"

"The hole," as Sylvie called it, was indeed an immense gap in between the Boulevard Haussmann and the Boulevard des

Capucines, where the new home for the Paris Opera was under construction. The construction had begun several years before, and many said it would be the most beautiful opera house in the entire world. People were already calling it the Palais Garnier after Charles Garnier, the architect who had designed it. And it was Monsieur Garnier of whom Yvette Bertrand now spoke as if he were a personal friend. She had never even seen the man, let alone met him. But she studied the plans of the opera house in the newspapers as though she herself were the main client of the architect.

"I am not sure if the *pavillon* for the *abonnés* is correctly placed on the eastern side," she might say after perusing the plans in the newspaper one day. (The *abonnés* were the season ticket holders and they had their own *pavillon*, or entrance, to the theater.) Or sometimes, she might sound more like an engineer. "The drainage has always been terrible on that southwest corner of the square. I hope they fix it." Or Yvette Bertrand might fancy herself an art critic. "For a statue in the *grand foyer*, they've hired a sculptor who is a woman! Have you ever heard of such a thing? I saw a picture of one of her statues in the newspaper. It was just so-so."

But now Madame Bertrand was raising her voice over the lashing wind in order to continue her opinion of the examination. "Look, Sylvie, you can still be in the second act of *Giselle* on Wednesday." Sylvie felt her mother's gaze. She knew her frown dimple had flashed. "Now don't give me that look, Sylvie—this is money. We need the money."

"Sorry, Mama," Sylvie replied. Her mother was right. They did need the money. Sylvie's father had died years before and her mother took a job as a laundress to support Sylvie and her older sister, Chantal. In the past six months, two of Yvette's wealthiest—but very elderly—customers had died. This had substantially cut into their income, and so far she had not been able to find two new customers willing to pay as much as Madame Hertier and Monsieur Moiret.

The second act of *Giselle,* when the spirits, the Wilis, rose from their graves, was the most beautiful and mystical part of the ballet. But Sylvie knew that she would be little more than a decoration—stage furniture, she called it. In certain ballets, the little rats were often put onstage and functioned more like scenery than actual dancers. Had she been advanced to the second level, she *could* have been in the village scene as one of the throngs of maidens winding through the street. It did not require much dancing, but at least she could *move,* instead of standing in one place for twenty minutes, as rooted as a tree.

"But, Mama," Sylvie complained. "The measuring stick at the school said I was not even four feet eleven and a quarter inches, and when we measure at home it says *definitely* that I am four feet eleven and a quarter."

"Sylvie, dear, when we measure you at home we stand you on the warped kitchen floor and make a mark against the door. It can never be as accurate as the measuring instruments at the ballet school." Madame Bertand stopped short. "Just take a

[11]

look at that building where we live. There's not a straight line in it. See how it leans?"

They had just turned into the Rue Saint-Martin. Sylvie observed that the apartment building they lived in did in fact lean, like an old man on a cane. Sylvie could never understand how a building made of stone could tilt but her mother had told her it had something to do with the foundation, and where they lived in Paris — Le Marais, which meant "swamp." Yes, their neighborhood had once been a swamp, which explained why the foundations settled and buildings tipped. Theirs was not the only crooked one in Le Marais.

Madame Bertrand squeezed her daughter's hand. "Try not to worry, Sylvie. They do not always stick to the rules about height. I will go to Monsieur Perrot and discuss the possibility that in a month or two, if you still haven't grown, you might be considered, because of your strength, for advancement."

"No, Mama. That would be too embarrassing."

"Why would it be embarrassing?"

"That would be like Madame du Bac."

"Sylvie, I am nothing like Madame du Bac and you know it."

"But Monsieur Perrot . . ." Sylvie sighed, unable to find the right words to explain her objections. "It's just, Mama . . ."

"Just what? He is the master teacher. He is the one who can make the final decisions. And you are a hard worker, Sylvie. Everyone knows that."

[12]

They turned into the small courtyard that led to the door of their building.

"I must go see Madame Tatou." Sylvie's mother nodded toward the doorway of their landlady. "And pay her what I owe for rent. Maybe she has some mending for me to do. You go upstairs and put the kettle on." She handed Sylvie the large brass key.

Sylvie took it and bounded up the stairs. She would measure herself against the door once more just to be sure. As she ran up the four flights of stairs she wondered if it was sinful to pray for three-quarters.

Just three little quarter inches, three measly quarters, she thought. *Lord, haven't people prayed for worse?*

Chapter 2

Sylvie unlocked the door, untied the ribbons of her bonnet, flung it on the table, then raced for the measuring door. She had done this so many times she did not even need help. There was a thin piece of very stiff paper that she would place on top of her head as she stood as straight as she could against the door. She would then step away and see how it compared to the marks she had made just that morning, before school. She knew it was ridiculous. She couldn't have grown since this morning, but she knew she hadn't shrunk, either—as the school measuring stick suggested.

She was so intent on her task that she did not notice, in the shadows of the kitchen, the rather shapeless heap on a stool in the corner. But then Sylvie smelled wet clothing, cut by a more acrid smell. The light in the kitchen was very dim, especially on a dark, rainy day, but Sylvie saw the red glowing point. Before she could say anything, the heap spoke.

"Still too short, eh?" The scent of cheap perfume swirled through the air.

"Chantal!"

"*Non!* The empress!" the voice replied sarcastically.

"What are you doing here?"

"I came to see my dear mama and very short little sister. Hi, stubby," she snorted as she took a puff on her cigarette.

But Sylvie knew this was not the real reason Chantal was visiting. She had come to see her *dear mama* for money.

"She doesn't have any, Chantal," Sylvie replied, ignoring the insult. "She is just paying the rest of the rent right now."

"No new customers since Madame Hertier kicked off?"

Sylvie couldn't stand to hear her sister talk like this. She knew she should be used to it. But she never was.

"You shouldn't smoke in here. It hurts Mama's lungs." Sylvie took a cloth and began waving it about, attempting to clear the air. She snapped the cloth willfully, as if to take out her frustrations on the wisps of smoke from Chantal's cigarette.

"Sorry." Chantal rose from the stool and walked toward a flowerpot that, in the dimness of the apartment, had put forth an anemic rose. Button roses, they were called. Chantal ground out the cigarette stub in the dirt of the pot. "Monsieur Gregory used to have these put into the bouquets he sent me. How is that Italian hussy he now fancies?"

At that precise moment, their mother walked in. "Hussy? Who's a hussy?" she asked. She twitched her nose like a rabbit as she sniffed the telltale traces of Chantal's cigarette.

"All the Italians, if you ask me," Chantal replied. "They will be the ruin of the Paris Opera Ballet *and* the school. The Italians get all the roles."

"Nonsense. *You* got kicked out of the opera because you were lazy! Not because you weren't Italian."

"And you, Mama? There were no Italians when you were in the ballet. What was *your* reason for leaving?"

Sylvie held her breath. How could Chantal be so cruel? It was not the same at all! Their mother had not been dismissed from the ballet. Sylvie had never been quite sure *why* her mother had left, but she certainly had not been forced to leave.

Yvette Bertrand turned on her elder daughter in a fury. She raised her hand to slap Chantal. But then she actually grabbed her own hand to stay it.

"Hmmph!" Chantal said, and shrugged. A triumphant little smile curled across her face.

Sylvie looked at her mother. Her face was white. Her black eyes blazed. Why had Chantal baited her like this? Sylvie had known since she was little not to speak about her mother's time at the ballet. It always made her mother very sad to talk about her own dancing. She had become a member of the *corps* but then, for reasons she never really explained, had to leave suddenly.

However, Sylvie knew that her mother had never forgiven Chantal for being kicked out. She was dismissed not for lack of talent, but for sheer laziness. And she had already made it into the *coryphée*, the second rank in the Paris Opera Ballet. But now she was dancing in a dance hall, Les Jolies Gamines. Sylvie knew her mother was absolutely humiliated.

When Chantal had been told to leave, their mother had raged and said it was the worst thing that had ever happened to her in her entire life. "Worse than when Papa died?" Sylvie had asked. Her mother had given her an odd stare but didn't answer.

The question seemed to be left hanging in the air forever. This response — or lack of it — made a deep impression on Sylvie. The very next day, the day she had turned seven, her mother had taken her to enroll in the school of ballet. Sylvie knew from that moment on she must never disappoint her mother as Chantal had.

And she wouldn't. She was not lazy. She loved to dance. She loved everything about it, even dressing her bruised and often bloody toes after long hours of class.

She looked at her mother and Chantal now — both such determined women. Sylvie hoped that this was not going to turn into one of their big fights. When these fights happened, Sylvie simply tried to become invisible. She would shrink back into the shadows of the tiny apartment. Her mother and sister could fight over the stupidest things. And there was no reasoning with them when they did.

There was Chantal's hideously dyed red hair, her smoking in public, her cheap friends, and on and on. Italian ballerinas were the least of it. But Sylvie knew it was true that, in the last few years, the Paris Opera Ballet, the directors of the school, and the teachers had developed a passion for Italians. Some blamed the new director and teacher of the advanced class; she was Italian and her predecessor, the great ballerina Marie Taglioni, had also been from Italy.

But who could argue that the adorable Giuseppina Bozzacchi had been the perfect choice to dance the role of Swanilda in *Coppélia*? Sylvie knew she had caused a sensation when this brand-new ballet had premiered in May. And she was only fifteen and as delicate in spirit as she was *en pointe*. And Sylvie was certain that she had not been cavorting about with Monsieur Gregory or any of the other *abonnés*, the gentlemen who often courted the ballerinas. These *affaires des coulisse*—the *coulisses* were the "wings of the stage"—as the gossip columnists called the romances, usually ended in disaster. (There were the rare exceptions, such as Count Ludovic Lepic, who was passionately devoted to Marie Sanlaville. He had not only provided her with an elaborate apartment in a very fancy neighborhood but also constantly showered her with gifts.)

"But I think Giuseppina is quite wonderful," Sylvie dared offer. "Perhaps not as good for the part as Léontine Beaugrand would have been . . ." Léontine was another principal dancer whom Sylvie admired.

"Your beloved Beaugrand will not advance one bit with the Italians about," Chantal said.

It was probably true. For even though Léontine Beaugrand was a soloist and embodied the very best of the restrained style of the French tradition, the fickle audiences were now enamored of only the Italian ballerinas. Or almost anyone foreign.

"It's not the Italians you need to worry about!" Yvette said, raising her voice to an alarming level.

Sylvie opened her eyes wide. "Who do we have to worry about?"

"The Prussians!"

"Ah, yes! The Prussians!" Chantal said with a studied gravity. She then squared her shoulders and, holding her chin high, said, "You see, Sylvie, there is more to worry about than your precious three-quarters of an inch."

"What are you talking about?" Sylvie looked at both her mother and Chantal. It was as if she were being left out of some grand secret. She hated this feeling. But her mother had turned her back, and now Chantal flounced toward the door, her shrill red curls bouncing as she dragged her somewhat tattered dignity behind her.

That night, Sylvie could not sleep. One minute she was wondering what Prussians were exactly and the next she was worried about, as Chantal had said, "her precious three-quarters of an inch."

Well, she couldn't do anything about the Prussians, whoever they were, but she had a new idea about growing. It did not seem right, Sylvie decided, to pray to God to be taller. But maybe she could stretch herself some way?

Her mother was sound asleep, so, very carefully, Sylvie crawled out of the bed they shared.

High up on a wall were two hooks where her mother strung cord to hang laundry. Sylvie took the ball of cord, the end of which was clipped with the stub of a broken clothespin, and strung it twice between the hooks. The cord would certainly hold her when doubled. After all, she didn't weigh that much more than a pile of wet laundry. She quietly moved a chair over and climbed up, then pulled firmly with both hands on the cord. The hooks didn't budge. *All right! Here I go,* she thought. She swung out on the laundry line away from the chair and hung. Her feet were several inches above the floor.

She closed her eyes and tried to visualize her muscles stretching longer. If the muscles stretched did that mean that the bones would have to stretch as well, to keep up with the muscles? An interesting question. And how much could she stretch herself, say, in a week? A quarter inch? How long was that exactly? Half the length of that broken clothespin? No, much smaller, but also not as tiny as the ladybug that had lighted on her shoulder when she had walked by the flower seller last week. Her hands began to burn and her shoulders grew tired, but Sylvie kept hanging. She would think of other things. *Let's see, clothespins, ladybugs — Prussians. What exactly are Prussians? And why should we worry about them?* Her shoulders really ached now. She hoped it was worth it. *And am I getting longer? Taller? Why does one sometimes say longer and other times taller? Does it matter?*

Before Sylvie could answer that question, she dropped from the clothesline with a soft thud. She resisted measuring herself again. She would try hanging from the line a few more times, perhaps next time with weights on her feet. Yes, she could tie on bags of flour that would pull her down even more. She spit on the palms of her hands, which were still burning, and went back to bed.

Chapter 3

As Sylvie and her mother made their way to the Rue le Peletier the next day, Sylvie noticed small clots of people on the corners, their brows creased in worry as they talked rapidly. Was it the Prussians they were talking about?

The rain earlier in the week had finally ceased and the sky was brilliant. *"Un bleu éclat,"* her mother had exclaimed, and clapped her hands in a literal declaration of the "clapping blue" sky. The expression, however, did not match the mood of Paris; it might as well have been a somber, drizzly day in November and not sunny June. The faces of pedestrians were gripped with fear and apprehension. So subdued was the mood that tempers that normally would have found a dozen flashpoints — slop pails inconsiderately emptied onto pathways, jams of horse carts with drivers yelling at one another — seemed to have been extinguished.

It was as if, in the course of a day, everything had changed for Sylvie. The city, the ballet, her life. That morning her mother had tried to explain it all. It had something to do with

a German prince who had an unpronounceable name—
Hollyholling or something. "Tell me again, Mama: What is
this place called Prussia?" Sylvie asked.

Yvette herself was unsure.

"It's a country or bunch of little countries. They call
them states, I think, and they have something to do with
Germany."

"But where's Germany?"

"Someplace east."

"Far to the east?"

"I don't know, Sylvie. You are asking me too many questions."

"But what does a prince have to do with it?"

"He's supposed to become king of Spain. I'm not sure
why. But France doesn't like it."

Sylvie's head was swirling. Prussia, Germany, Spain? Why
did these countries care about some prince?

"Mama, why should we care? What business is it of ours?"

"Don't ask me, *ma petite*. Don't bother yourself with talk
of war. Just keep your mind on *your* business. Dancing!"

That was Sylvie's business. But recently, as her mother had
also explained, there had been talk of closing down the Paris
Opera Ballet temporarily, and a suspension of all classes due
to these rumblings of war. Such a thing had never happened.
Sylvie's life was the ballet. She knew nothing else, really. Since
she was seven years old, it was all that she had done. Get up

each morning, six days a week, at six. Eat whatever scant breakfast her mother could make — usually a slice of bread (if there had been money that week, with some marmalade) and a bowl of coffee with milk, again if there had been money. Then off for the long walk to the opera house, as they were now doing. Or if there was money, they would take a trolley.

If it was a Monday, Wednesday, or Friday, and if she was lucky, Sylvie would be informed if there was a small role for her in that evening's performance — a "stage furniture" role at best. That would mean twenty extra *sous* in her pocket. Then class would begin. There would be absolute silence except for the music of a violin or a piano. She would dance until the noon lunch break. Some girls went home if they lived nearby. Sylvie would eat the bit of bread saved from breakfast and the cheese that her mother made sure she always had.

That was her life. That was the life of every *petit rat*. There was no school for learning other things such as reading, mathematics, or history. There was no need to learn other things. As far as Sylvie was concerned, the opera house contained a universe. It was where magic was made. Forests were constructed out of fake trees, their quivering leaves blown by great bellows. Skies were pricked with stars made from a special kind of light called limelight. There were rushing "waterfalls" and shimmering "ponds," "mountains" and lush "gardens" that bloomed with flowers made of velvet, silk, and sometimes paper. Who needed the so-called real world when one of greater beauty and absolute perfection was held within the Paris Opera? And what a contradiction it was that the opera house itself, although considered so ugly on the outside, contained such beauty within.

There were no bad smells in the opera house, at least not like the ones Sylvie was now smelling as she crossed the Rue Jean-Jacques Rousseau. And the trees here were not nearly as pretty, Sylvie thought, glancing at the few spindly ones along the way. And the sun was much too bright. Why, it didn't even look like the sun. It was not round and butter yellow at all, the way a sun should be. It was instead an ugly smear of white in the sky that hurt one's eyes.

Why was some country called Prussia—stupid, stupid name for a country—about to spoil all this? It was ridiculous.

Sylvie pressed her lips together. Her frown dimple flashed. She was not about to let this Prussia interfere with her business. And today she had some very specific business. *Today I will ask Mademoiselle Léontine! I will, I will, I will!*

As the welcome shadows of the opera house reached out for her, Sylvie thrust out her chin. She would not waver in her task. She would not let the rumors of war distract her. This was more important. She had been promising herself for weeks to ask Léontine Beaugrand if she would be her *petite mère*, or "little mother."

It was crucial to have a *petite mère*. Almost every little rat had one. The *petites mères* were better than teachers, to Sylvie's mind. They rarely scolded. When you were feeling as if nothing would ever go right, as if your feet would never work correctly, the *petites mères* told you stories of *their* days as little rats. They helped you go on. And perhaps most important of all, if they thought you showed promise or had been unfairly overlooked by a teacher, they spoke to a grand teacher—one who taught the advanced classes—or perhaps even a choreographer.

Sylvie knew that she must have a *petite mère*. She had been too shy to ask, but she had to be done with that. Shyness counted for nothing. And that horrible Marie du Bac, just two days before, had asked none other than Eugénie Fiocre to be her *petite mère.* And Eugénie had accepted! There was no telling how quickly Marie would move along now, especially since that Monsieur Degas had decided to use her as a model for his sculpture. Marie was perfectly proportioned, and her back curved in just the tiniest bit, which was said to account for great suppleness.

She was indeed supple. Sylvie would give her that. But she was technically very sloppy. As long as Monsieur Degas asked her to stand still she would be fine, but when doing an *entrechat* or a *port de bras*—she might as well be a circus performer. (Not that Sylvie had ever seen a circus performer. She only knew that the acrobats and trapeze performers were considered clumsy and coarse compared to ballerinas.)

Sylvie told herself again that this morning she would ask

Mademoiselle Léontine. The rule was that a *petit rat* had to ask for herself. Her mother could not do it for her, nor could a friend. Sylvie would do it herself and she had planned out just how she would do it. She knew that Mademoiselle Léontine always took a cup of tea just following lunch, in a small room off one of the costume workshops. Sylvie planned to go there just before the break was finished and ask to speak with her. She had reviewed this plan with her mother, who thought it was good, and they had even rehearsed exactly what Sylvie was going to say.

Silently, the words ran through her head as she and her mother turned the corner into the Rue de la Grange Batelière and walked quickly toward the back entrance of the opera house. *"Pardon me, Mademoiselle Beaugrand, for interrupting your tea . . ."* She and her mother, of course, had fretted over whether to call it tea, since what Léontine drank was actually hot water with lemon juice. But it sounded very peculiar to say "pardon me for interrupting your hot water and lemon juice."

They walked by the *concierge du théâtre* in the entrance hall, who nodded at them. Then they continued up stairs and began to thread their way through a maze of rooms called collectively the *foyer de la danse*. The *foyer* contained rooms for rehearsing and taking classes. But it was not strictly reserved for dancers, teachers, and musicians. The season ticket holders were permitted to mingle with the dancers in these spaces, and it was here that many a romantic liaison was started between a beautiful but impoverished young dancer and a gentleman.

Sylvie's mother *always* accompanied her through these public spaces. There were strict rules as to when and how many mothers could enter the classroom when the lesson was in progress. And as much as Yvette Bertrand would have loved to watch every single minute of her daughter's class (especially today, with the distinguished Jules Perrot teaching), she knew that it was much more important for her to stay close to her daughter in these public places. Many mothers did not care.

Sylvie had been looking down at the floor of the corridor, but then she heard her mother's tiny gasp and felt the sudden pressure of her hand. She stopped and when she looked up, Mademoiselle Léontine stood before them.

She was tall and had thick, luxuriant hair that reminded Sylvie of dark, almost burned honey. Her eyes were a smoky, undefinable color, and she had a small mole on her right cheek. Now it was Sylvie's turn to gasp. What was Léontine doing here? The soloists never came in this early.

"Why, Sylvie, is everything all right?" Léontine Beaugrand chuckled. "My goodness! It looks as if you have seen a ghost. I hope I did not shock you."

That could be the understatement of the year, Sylvie thought. She felt the pressure of her mother's hand increase. There was something that seemed to be communicated in that hand roughened by years of harsh soap and scalding water. *Now or never!* That was the message.

There was not another soul around, not within thirty feet. This in itself was somewhat of a miracle because more than seven thousand people worked within the salons, workshops, and rehearsal halls of the opera. It was, in truth, an enormous factory devoted to manufacturing the magic of the theater.

Sylvie gulped and looked straight into Léontine Beaugrand's earnest eyes. *Are they gray or tawny brown?* she wondered. "Mademoiselle Léontine, I would be most honored if you would consider being my *petite mère*. I have worked very hard," Sylvie said breathlessly.

"Oh, that I know, my dear. I have seen you in class many times."

She noticed me! Sylvie thought. *She actually noticed me? Oh, I hope it wasn't when I was making a mess out of my* fouettés *the other day. I looked like a windmill on a rampage.*

"I know I am short. But I think I will grow. I hope so."

"Oh, so do I," Mademoiselle Léontine replied with a twinkle in her eye.

Is she saying yes or no? Sylvie could feel her mother growing tense beside her.

"But you know," Mademoiselle Léontine continued, "one must not only grow in height but in spirit, Sylvie."

Sylvie's heart began to sink. Something inside her stomach seemed to turn dark. She cast her eyes to the floor. She was being rejected. She felt hot tears forming behind her eyelids. This was as bad as war; she was sure. Let the Prussians come. There was no life left for her. She was in such complete despair she did not hear Léontine Beaugrand's next words.

"But I see seeds of great spirit. I cannot make you grow, but I can nurture those seeds of spirit."

Sylvie's mother was actually poking her in the ribs now. Sylvie looked up.

"Yes, I will be your *petite mère*." Léontine smiled gently at Sylvie and took her hand. "It will be my pleasure. Now run along, my dear, and don't be late for class."

Sylvie was so stunned she forgot to say thank you. She and her mother proceeded to the dressing room in a fog of euphoria. The things that usually annoyed her did not this morning. Marie du Bac was already claiming the best pair of pink slippers from last week's performance, declaring that they rightfully belonged to her because her *petite mère*, Eugénie Fiocre, had danced in them. Sylvie simply didn't care. And, for the first time in months, she even forgot about that infuriating three-quarters of an inch she lacked to be five feet. She began changing into her class *tutu*.

"Mama," she called. "Help me with the sash." Sylvie's fingers were shaking so hard with excitement that she had made a mess of the bow, the tails of which had to be a strict regulation length—no shorter than eight inches, no longer than ten, and not a fraction less or more. When her sash was properly tied, Sylvie went to the powder box, took a puff, and powdered her arms and hands with a bit of white to make them look more graceful. Then she peered hard at herself in the mirror. "Mademoiselle Léontine is to be my *petite mère*," she whispered. She made a slow *pirouette* in front of the mirror to make sure that there were no wrinkles in her skirt before going into the classroom.

At the door of the classroom, she and her mother stopped in front of a box with ground rosin. As Sylvie dipped her slippers into the rosin, she watched the little puffy clouds swirl up. She liked the slightly sharp scent. The rosin would prevent her from slipping. But so happy was she this morning that she felt she could never fall.

Chapter 4

As Sylvie was dipping her toes into the rosin box, her mother hovered close by and whispered, "You packed that extra bread I gave you in your satchel, Sylvie?"

"Yes, Mama. Don't worry."

Sylvie knew it was not just the extra bread her mother was worrying about. Nearby, a girl of about fifteen with almost white-blond hair was begging ten *sous* for some sweets from a potbellied gentleman. Sylvie saw her mother looking at the girl through narrowed eyes. It was a common sight. Chantal had been guilty of this. And as her mother said with monotonous regularity, Chantal had made a big fat mess out of her life.

There were no other words for it. Chantal was tall, unlike Sylvie, and she had a beautiful line when she danced and a deep feeling for music. Why, Sylvie often wondered, had her sister not taken advantage of all of this? If she herself had the seeds of a large spirit, as Mademoiselle Léontine had said, then Chantal had the sludge of indolence.

"Don't worry, Mama," Sylvie said again, and gave her mother's hand a squeeze. "Please, Mama. Now go along. I will be fine."

Only two mothers at a time were permitted in the classroom itself. The others were required to sit in a neighboring room. It was not Yvette Bertrand's turn today. But as Sylvie walked into the classroom, she could feel her mother's eyes on her back. It wasn't just Chantal's failure that her mother rued. It was her own time as a dancer. Even when her mother was not there, Sylvie sometimes felt as if there was a ghost ballerina dancing near her, *plié*-ing at the *barre* alongside her. It was her mother, younger, slimmer, with no streaks of gray in her hair. It was as if she and her mother were locked in some spectral *pas de deux*. She often had to concentrate quite hard to rid herself of this feeling.

But today it would be easy. Today, within the space of a few minutes, she had acquired a *petite mère!* It was amazing, she thought, how things could change so quickly within such a short time. The day before, she had entered the classroom almost in tears after her failure. But then the world had been at peace and she had never heard of Prussians. Today she brimmed with happiness and hope, yet France was on the brink of war.

The only thing Sylvie thought could make this day more perfect would be if Monsieur Degas were there to paint her and not Marie du Bac. But as she entered she saw no tall silk hat on the floor, no man sitting in the corner with a sketch pad.

Sun poured through the window and the studio was already hot, so the girls had avoided the spaces at the *barre* that were in direct sunlight. But Sylvie always liked to do her *barre* work in the sun. The shadow she printed on that oblong plank of sunshine that came through the window was always elegant. It was as if there were two mirrors: the real mirror that reflected her as she was; and the second, that plank of sunshine printed with her shadow, showing what she might become—if only she would grow.

Today's class, the Friday class, would be taught by Jules Perrot, who was not just a dance teacher but a choreographer as well. For this Sylvie was greatly relieved. Madame Théodore had been in a horrid mood all week.

Some were still adjusting the ribbons of their slippers as the teacher entered.

"Bonjour, monsieur le maître."

Ten girls curtsied deeply and delicately touched the edge of their *tutus*, which came to mid calf.

Monsieur Perrot was a man of medium height who wore his white hair combed straight back. When he blinked, there was something about his eyes that reminded Sylvie of a tortoise. Not that she had ever seen a tortoise in real life. But once in the scenery shop she had watched as carpenters constructed one for an opera.

After curtsying, they went to the *barre* to begin the first part of the class. The violinist began playing a slow, languorous piece of music picked especially for the warm-up. When the ballet master tapped the long stick he held for marking the counts, the class officially began. All the students faced forward in second position and bent their knees in a *demi-plié*. This was Sylvie's least favorite part of class. It seemed slow and tedious. But she tried to let the music seep into her mind, her muscles, her very bones.

Soon the warm-up was over and it was time for the next phase of the *barre* work. Sylvie wanted to do her best. She must be prepared if Mademoiselle Léontine came into the class to watch. Eugénie Fiocre was there and watching Marie du Bac like a hawk.

The tempo of the music increased as the class began the *battements tendus* in which one foot slides across the floor, stretching to a point. This was a strengthening exercise for fast and precise footwork later.

Monsieur Perrot tapped the long baton he carried in time to the music. His eyes rested on Sylvie. First he checked her posture and then he looked down to her feet. She was trying to flick them as quickly and neatly as possible. Sylvie was self-conscious about her feet. She did not have the beautiful arch that her sister had. The shape of a foot was of key importance, but there was not much that could be done to change it. Therefore she must work doubly hard to strengthen her feet. It was a relief when they moved on to *battements frappés* in which the ball of the foot strikes the floor sharply. Sylvie felt that this exercise did not reveal her clumsy foot shape as much as the previous *battements*.

She had been concentrating so hard she did not notice until it was time for center work that Mademoiselle Léontine had entered the classroom. Center work *had* to be better than yesterday, when she'd been as floppy as a rag doll. Or a corpse, as Madame Théodore had so kindly described her.

Marie du Bac pushed in front of her so she could be in the first row, clearly in view of Eugénie Fiocre. Turning to Sylvie, Isabel muttered, *"Quelle imbécile vaniteuse!"* A vain imbecile! Yes, that was Marie du Bac. Well, maybe not so much of an imbecile. But her pushing in front seemed so vain to Sylvie. She vowed she would never try to show off for Mademoiselle Léontine.

"Flûte!" Isabel softly whispered an almost-but-not-quite swear word. Sylvie suppressed a chuckle.

As soon as Sylvie took her place in the center, she knew she did not look like "a corpse," although she was blocked by Marie du Bac. Everything felt aligned, in balance. The real test was not the *arabesques* or the *tendus* but the slow, sustained movements, the adagio steps, the leg extensions. And today the *développé* that she had butchered yesterday became something entirely different. Sylvie felt her leg unfold as if it were emerging from some hidden place, as if a flower had bloomed. Yes, it was as if a miraculous blossom had mysteriously appeared in thin air. And this blossom that just happened to be her leg was caressing the space around her.

Her leg began to journey upward, through *passé,* to a full

extension so high that if there had been stars in the classroom she could have reached them.

And now dancers were called forward, three at a time, to perform a short combination that included a *pirouette*. Sylvie had never done more than two *pirouettes* in a row. She felt Mademoiselle Léontine looking straight at her. Sylvie told herself that she would be very happy to do two perfect *pirouettes*. She went into the first *pirouette*. She was balanced *en pointe* on one foot and whipped the other around. Then the second. She had not even completed the second when she thought, almost unconsciously, *Oh, I can go around again.* It was as if another force had possessed her, a force that allowed her, inspired her to do this third rotation. She had no fear, no second thoughts. It was beyond her control. She was just doing it!

"Wow!" Isabel whispered when Sylvie was done.

Sylvie blinked. "I don't know what happened."

"I know what happened. You just did a triple!"

"I don't think it was me. It was something outside of me." Sylvie looked down at her shoes. "I think it was the shoes. Yes, I think so. They are quite marvelous!" Sylvie silently vowed that she would wear these shoes until they fell apart completely.

When the class finally finished, the girls once more curtsied deeply to Monsieur Perrot and to the violinist, then clapped, to show their appreciation. By the time Sylvie finished clapping, she had noticed that Léontine Beaugrand was gone. This surprised her. She must have left very quickly.

But Marie du Bac was talking animatedly with Eugénie Fiocre, who was cupping Marie's face with her hands as if saying, "I adore you . . . you are the most wonderful dancer . . . I can see you in *Giselle* . . . yes, the *pas de deux* . . ."

Marie du Bac left the classroom arm in arm with Eugénie Fiocre. Then, turning to a girl named Bertine, she said carelessly over her shoulder, "Bertine, I must have lunch with Mademoiselle Fiocre today. Sorry . . . another day perhaps."

Sylvie wondered about Léontine. Did she feel that she had made a wrong choice in becoming Sylvie's *petite mère*? She had done a triple *pirouette*, after all, and during the *barre* work Sylvie had received two corrections. That was good. The more corrections one received the better, because it meant that Monsieur Perrot was paying attention to you. Some students received none. Marie had received three. But Sylvie didn't care. She was happier that Isabel had received four. And Sylvie herself had her triple. No one else had done that.

"Sylvie! Sylvie!" Her mother was running up to her outside the classroom. "They want you tonight for *Giselle*." Yvette's eyes were merry with a sparkling light.

"Oh, Mama, I have stood around as a peasant in *Giselle* a thousand times!"

"Sylvie, this is different. You are to be the statue on the gravestone."

Great! thought Sylvie. *Just what I always wanted to be — a statue of the Virgin Mary. Now I won't even be able to move!*

"Everyone will see you now. More clearly than if you were with a gaggle of peasant girls," Yvette Bertrand rattled on excitedly. "Monsieur Perrot choreographed that ballet. He is very particular about every detail. He must have seen something in you this morning."

"I did a triple *pirouette*," Sylvie said. *And now I will be a statue.*

"You did a triple? *Mon Dieu!* At your age I had never done a triple!"

"I think it was the shoes, Mama. They are really good."

"Nonsense!" Yvette exclaimed. "It was you."

"But Monsieur Perrot only gave me two corrections. Marie du Bac got three and Isabel four."

"Sylvie, *tais-toi!*" her mother hissed. "Quit complaining. Take the role. A *sou* is a *sou*. You will receive twenty tonight."

Sylvie shut her eyes tight and counted to five. Sometimes she thought she just might explode. "Mama, I know about the money. But it isn't really just the money, is it?" She stepped forward, closer to her mother. "Isn't it, Mama?" Sylvie challenged.

"I just want what's best for you, Sylvie." Her mother's voice quavered.

"No, Mama, you want me to make up for everything that Chantal never did!" As soon as the words were out, Sylvie felt

awful. "I'm sorry, Mama. I didn't mean to say that. Forget it."
She quickly linked arms with her mother and desperately tried
to think of another subject. "But, Mama, what happened to
Mademoiselle Léontine?"

"I don't know. She had to leave quickly. An emergency of
some sort. Someone came in and delivered a note to her and
she just . . . *phut!*" Yvette made a funny little sound by blowing
air out of her mouth.

"All right, Mama. I won't complain."

"Quickly now, *chérie*, to Madame Preschinka for your fitting. Just go, Sylvie." And her mother gave her a gentle push in
the direction of the costume department.

Chapter 5

The opening notes of music hung in the air, soft as the mist that rose from the stage. From a concealed trough in the floor, ten stagehands pumped bellows that blew beneath the swags of gauze. The footlights had been turned down and scrimmed so that the light was soft and mysterious.

Sylvie was standing atop a plaster tombstone in a gown with lead weights, to make it hang straight and immovable as stone. For that indeed was what she was supposed to be — a stone statue of the Virgin Mary on a grave, the grave of Giselle. Her face had been dusted a chalky gray. She was told to tip her chin up toward the moon and not to move a muscle. The moon was suspended by invisible string. What was invisible to the audience but not to Sylvie was the lighting man in the wings holding the limelight and directing it toward the silver-painted moon.

She must stand like this for the entire second act. It was as far removed from dancing as a dancer could be while still onstage.

The second act of *Giselle* takes place in a graveyard in a forest.

At the end of the first act, Giselle, the peasant girl, dies when she discovers that her beloved has lied to her about his true identity and is, in fact, engaged to another maiden.

Sylvie had been stage furniture in this ballet a half dozen times, always as a laughing peasant girl in the first act. But this time was entirely different. The feeling on the stage in the second act was the complete opposite of the liveliness and joy of the village. Now, the stillness and the slowly swirling tendrils of make-believe mist wound through the air like a long moan. The stage had become a haunted forest. Sylvie felt an eeriness begin to seep into her, stir her in ways she had never imagined. *Perhaps,* she wondered to herself, *I have never really thought about death.* It was all make-believe, of course, but here she was, a pretend statue on the pretend grave of a young, beautiful maiden. A dead maiden.

And she, Sylvie, who was not permitted to move, felt a tear begin to roll down her cheek. *I can't cry. Why am I crying?*

She heard a rustle backstage. It was the Wilis, getting ready for their entrance. The graveyard was haunted by the ghosts of young maidens who had died before their wedding day. These ghosts were called Wilis. A shiver ran up Sylvie's spine. She couldn't stop her tears. Why was she reacting this way?

She remembered what her *petite mère* had said that afternoon when she had returned to school and heard about Sylvie's part. "Sylvie, this is not bad. Not bad at all to be a statue. Do you realize that, perched on that gravestone, you are in the perfect position to watch? You do not need to move anything but your eyes. So you must watch the steps. It is not enough to know the steps by heart. There is more—steps are the words of dance. Steps are the language of ballet. They have accents, a music all their own. Every dancer inflects them differently."

But how can I watch them if I am crying? Dare I blink?

The music, quiet at first, gradually became louder, and the tempo quickened. And now Sylvie did blink as a misty figure shot from the wings in a *grand jeté*, followed by two more leaps. The audience gasped and then began applauding wildly. It was Giuseppina Bozzacchi in the role of Myrtha, the queen of the Wilis. Giuseppina soared across the stage. The pasteboard moon above trembled from the wind of her flight. Sylvie had never seen anything like it. There were no steps to watch as Giuseppina's feet barely seemed to touch the ground. Sylvie forgot her tears. She was simply hypnotized by what she was seeing.

The music slowed once more, and Giuseppina began an adagio sequence—slow and sustained steps and motions that flowed from one to another. Everything was seamless. Her body, her movements, were liquid. But she, Giuseppina Bozzacchi, was a creature of air.

She deserves the part, Sylvie thought. *She is extraordinary.* Adèle Lormier, who was in the role of Giselle, now rose as a ghost from behind the tombstone on which Sylvie stood. Adèle appeared clumsy and heavy by comparison. There was a series of *pas de bourrée* that both Giselle and Myrtha performed. As the two dancers rose onto their toes and began to travel across the stage, Adèle appeared as if she was stepping each time, but Giuseppina simply floated. *Monsieur Degas should paint her!* Sylvie thought. She had caught a glimpse of the artist in the second row, stage right.

When the curtain came down, Sylvie's head was swirling with steps and the accents that the dancers gave to those steps. Adèle Lormier's accent, if it could be called that, was monotone, but Giuseppina danced within a spectrum of inflections that was as delicate and varied as the colors of a rainbow.

After the final curtain call, Sylvie raced backstage, nearly bumping into two men who were moving a flat of scenery. She was looking for Léontine, but everything was chaos as the stagehands, under the cover of the thunderous applause, rushed to remove scenery from the stage.

One Wili was complaining loudly to another about a roach she had seen skittering across the stage just as she began a *glissade.*

"It was on stage left and heading right for the grave — not its, unfortunately, but Giselle's. Did you not see it?" She turned to Sylvie.

"No, no." Sylvie was still looking around, trying to search out Léontine.

"Oh, imagine if it had started to crawl up that gravestone and onto you! It would be hard to be a statue then." The two girls giggled.

"Yes, yes," Sylvie agreed. "Have you seen Léontine

Beaugrand?" But the two Wilis were rushing off, removing their headpieces.

"Move it, *chérie!*" another stagehand called. Sylvie was in his path as he came toward her with a huge reflector for the limelight.

"My toes!" moaned another Wili. She had plopped right down on the floor and was taking off her shoes. She drew out a blood-spotted wad of cotton. "Those *pas de bourrée* are killing me."

Sylvie finally managed to find Léontine Beaugrand backstage.

"What did you see? What did you think?" her *petite mère* asked eagerly.

"When Giuseppina danced, I saw color. I heard music that was not played by the musicians."

"Bravo, little one." Mademoiselle Léontine grasped Sylvie by the shoulders and gave her a kiss on each cheek. "You are a quick learner. I always knew that. Tomorrow, come early to the *foyer de la danse.* I will meet you for a little private instruction before classes commence. Should we practice *grands jetés?*"

Sylvie beamed. *I've been kissed by Léontine Beaugrand! I have a* petite mère *who thinks I am a quick learner. I have seen great dancing. I have stood like a statue, but inside I was always dancing. What could be better? My world is perfect!*

Sylvie knew that her mother was waiting for her by the stage door in the alley. She almost did not want to leave the opera house. There was nothing that could compare to this place of music and fantasy, of limelight and pasteboard moons, of *grands jetés* and the smell of the gaslights. This was her world. This was her passion.

But as Sylvie and her mother made their way through the sweltering heat of the June night, another world intruded. Fragments of heated conversation could be heard spilling from the sidewalk cafés and from passing pedestrians.

"The Prussians called our ambassador a pig! *Non!*"

"Not the Prussians. King William, the German king."

"It was Bismarck's meddling, believe me!"

"Yes, they say it was Bismarck who really wrote the telegram."

"There'll be war. Mark my words! War is coming."

"Because of a telegram?"

"Just an excuse. Time we showed those Prussians that French honor cannot be toyed with in this manner."

"War, Mama? Why war?" Sylvie asked.

Yvette clutched her daughter's hand and walked faster. She shook her head. "I don't know! Stupid! Some telegram. It's got everyone upset."

"Like the thing with the prince and the throne of Spain?"

"Yes, it is still about that, I believe," Yvette said vaguely. "Don't think about it. Tell me more about the performance."

And so Sylvie told her mother how Giuseppina flew across the stage. She told her about the flawless *demi-fouettés en l'air*. "Five in a row, Mama, just like this." And she raised her finger into the thick heat of the night and spun it around. "So she is an Italian with real talent." Sylvie paused. "Look, Mama! There she is, right over there on the corner! I am going to tell her myself how great she was."

Sylvie let go of her mother's hand and ran to the corner. "Giuseppina! Giuseppina!"

The ballerina turned and looked startled. She must not have recognized Sylvie at all. Of course they had never been in a class together, and the stars did not mingle much with the *petits rats*.

"It's me, the girl on the tombstone."

They both giggled at this introduction. *She laughs just like a little girl*, Sylvie thought. In fact, Sylvie realized Giuseppina Bozzacchi was quite small. Not *that* much bigger than herself. But she was terribly thin, and without her makeup, she looked extremely pale and fragile.

"I had to tell you. You were wonderful. You were like a bird . . . my . . . my heart almost stopped beating when you burst onto the stage with that *grand jeté*. I have never seen anything like it." Sylvie hoped she didn't sound stupid.

Giuseppina smiled. Her mouth almost seemed too large for her delicate face. She reached out and grasped Sylvie's hand. Her own hand was so thin it felt like chicken bones. She leaned forward, her eyes suddenly twinkling. "That is so kind of you. It is only gentlemen who ever really compliment me. The French ballerinas . . ." She hesitated. "Well, you know . . ." She paused again. Her Italian-accented French sounded musical.

"I know," Sylvia said. "But I don't care if you are Italian. I don't even care if you are Prussian." At this, they both broke out in gales of laughter.

"You are too charming! What is your name again?"

Sylvie realized that she had never introduced herself. "Sylvie. Sylvie Bertrand. But I am just a little rat. I am not even in the *quadrille* yet. Too short."

"Oh, no, no, no. You have a big heart. You will dance with a big heart, and no one will care how short you are."

"Really?"

"Really, Sylvie! Believe me. I must go now, but thank you, Sylvie Bertrand. Thank you so much." Sylvia watched the tiny ballerina as she headed down the Rue Richer and turned the corner at the intersection.

She was still in a daze as her mother walked up to the corner. "She is so kind, Mama, so little and so kind. She is not much bigger than me, is she?"

"I was noticing that, dear."

"She said I must dance with a big heart and no one will see how small I am."

"Oh, my, what a night you have had, Sylvie Bertrand!" her mother exclaimed. "Now, tell me more about what Mademoiselle Léontine said."

So Sylvie began to tell her mother everything that her *petite mère* had said to her. When she almost got to the end, Sylvie paused dramatically. "And . . . you know what else?"

"What else, Sylvie? What else?"

"She wants me to come early tomorrow, before class, for private instruction, Mama!"

"Oh, Sylvie!" Yvette Bertrand gasped with sheer delight. "Oh, my Sylvie! This is wonderful. I feel our luck is turning. Don't worry about how tall you are, for goodness' sake. With Léontine Beaugrand as your *petite mère*, I really don't believe your height will matter."

Sylvie felt a twinge as she saw her mother's eyes fill. She knew how hard it had been for her. She sometimes tried to imagine what it had been like to, within the space of barely one day, experience the birth of a daughter and the loss of a husband. For in fact, Sylvie's father had died on the very eve of her being born. With his death the family had been left nearly penniless.

When her father had died Sylvie knew that her mother had given up any hope for a comfortable life. She had given up the possibility of a decent bottle of wine on her table, or even three good meals every day, for after all, her father had been a butcher and could get meat cheap. But none of this seemed to matter to Yvette. She didn't need money, or food, or good wine if her dream of Sylvie's dancing in the Paris Opera Ballet came true. Who needed such things if one's daughter was a *danseuse*!

And now today she, Sylvie, had taken one step closer to fulfilling that dream. And despite her own great joy at having a *petite mère*, Sylvie felt something shudder deep within her. It was hard being another person's dream. And Sylvie knew she was just this. She was her mother's sustenance — her food, her wine — her hope.

When they returned to their apartment, they both went directly to bed. A gas lamp in the street outside let in a sliver of light through the one window of their apartment. Sylvie slept in the place next to the wall. She had on the floor a pair of toe shoes that were rumored to have been danced in by Léontine Beaugrand in *La Sylphide*. She didn't know for sure. But now with Mademoiselle Léontine as her *petite mère* she could ask her for an old pair herself. Next to the toe shoes was a picture of Marie Taglioni, the opera's greatest dancer ever, who had just this summer retired as the director. She was so worshipped by audiences that it was said her fans once made a soup from her old toe shoes.

Sylvie yawned. *I must ask Mademoiselle Léontine if I might have a picture of her to put up next to Taglioni. Ah, tomorrow. I cannot wait until tomorrow.*

Chapter 6

Sylvie was so excited that she rose before it was even light out. And when her mother woke she sat up in bed and blinked at her daughter, who was dangling with both hands from a clothesline double strung between two hooks.

"What in heaven's name are you doing, Sylvie Bertrand?"

"Stretching myself. I think it might work, Mama. I tried it the other night when you were asleep. I just thought before class today I would try it again." Sylvie smiled and with her bare feet flicking through the first morning light did a midair series of *battements,* then *tendus.* Her mother giggled.

After a scant breakfast they left for the opera house. Paris seemed oddly quiet and empty. Even at this early hour, the streets were usually filled with the noise of the city waking up: the creaking of wheels, the braying of cart animals protesting the whips of their drivers, the sounds of shutters being flung open. But now an unusual silence had settled on all the neighborhoods.

"What is this?" Yvette Bertrand said as she stepped

over refuse on the steps leading up to the back entrance of the opera house. Usually the custodian had made sure that the sweepers had cleared the steps well before students began to arrive. And the entrance itself was locked. They were early, yes, but not that early. Sylvie and her mother did not quite know what to do. They stood awkwardly on the steps, looking about. Several minutes passed, then a quarter of an hour, and then half an hour. Still no one came. And the Rue de la Grange Batelière seemed very empty. Sylvie could stand it no longer.

"I am going around to the Rue le Peletier to the other doors, Mama. This is so strange."

"All right. I shall wait here in case someone comes."

Sylvie disappeared around the corner of the building. Within two minutes, she was back. She looked deathly pale. "Mama, there is war."

"War?" Yvette Bertrand shook her head as if to clear it.

"Yes, madame. War." A street sweeper appeared, leaning on his broom. "The emperor has already left for the front." His accent was odd. Sylvie wondered what country he came from.

"The emperor? What front?" her mother asked.

"Well, madame, it is not Napoléon Bonaparte. Remember, he is dead. It is Napoléon III and the front is not Waterloo. It is Alsace. You little rats better become street rats. No more time for ballet. We must all prepare." His long nose curved down and nearly met his lip. When he grinned, his mouth, a narrow slot, revealed dark stubs of teeth. A cigarette hung from one corner of the slot.

"But why is the opera house closed?" Yvette demanded.

The sweeper threw down the cigarette in disgust. "Madame. It is just as I say. There is not time for these *bourgeois* follies—ballet, opera, art, *phut!*" He spat the sound out. "We must all prepare. If the Prussians begin to march west, and just suppose they take Paris, you think you can dance your way out of that mess? Ah, *non! Non! Non!*" He shook his finger at Sylvie and Yvette as a teacher might scold children. But he didn't look like any teacher. He reminded Sylvie of a mangy, skinny cat. His tilting greenish eyes were almost transparent.

Sylvie took a deep breath. Her voice cracked as she began to speak. "But you don't understand, monsieur," Sylvie said. "I was to have private instruction with Mademoiselle Léontine Beaugrand."

"I don't think so, *ma petite*." The sweeper smiled smugly and shook his head slowly. "I don't think so. The opera is closed until further notice." He picked up his broom, put it on his shoulder, and sauntered off.

Yvette stared at him hard. Her eyes narrowed. Sylvie had never seen such hatred in her mother's eyes.

"Mama, are you all right?"

"No," she answered sharply. Yvette wheeled around and took Sylvie by the shoulders. Sylvie was frightened. Her mother's eyes were blazing. Her face was masklike and scorched with rage.

"Mama?"

"Listen to me, Sylvie. I know this type of man. He is one of those filthy *communards*. I have heard talk of this kind. They are dreamless men and women. They know nothing of beauty, of art, of music, dance. They move through life to the monotonous rhythms of their shabby brooms and the noise of bleating work animals . . . and . . . and"—she hesitated—"they are dangerous."

"Dangerous, Mama? How can they be dangerous? Merely because they don't like art?"

"They can, believe me! They are revolutionaries, Sylvie! Revolutionaries."

"Is that so bad, Mama?"

"It is the worst. They want to turn everything upside down, and believe me, they are looking for this war as an excuse to do just that!"

Yvette Bertrand's eyes suddenly softened. Their darkness blurred behind a scrim of tears. Still, something lurked behind the tears. A nervousness, an uncertainty.

"Mama?" Sylvie said softly, and leaned closer.

Her mother drew out a handkerchief and pressed it to her nose and mouth almost as if to stop any sound, any word from escaping. "Sylvie." Her face crumbled.

"What is it, Mama? You can tell me. I love you."

"I have never told you this before. You see, your father thought I was so foolish when I enrolled Chantal in the opera ballet school. He would not allow any talk of it in the household. You have to understand that although your father always provided well for us before he died, he was one of those dreamless men."

"Didn't you love him, Mama?" Sylvie looked at her mother.

Tears were streaking down Yvette's face now. "He was a butcher, Sylvie." She gasped the words, as if this explained everything. But it didn't. Sylvie was more confused than ever now.

"But you married him."

"I know, I know, and every evening he came home still stained with the blood of the animals he had been cutting up all day long. He smelled of blood. That is how I started as a laundress. I washed his butcher's aprons and tunics and those of the other men." She blew her nose and looked at Sylvie. "Sylvie, he was a good man. But he did not know music or art. He moved to the rhythms of a butcher's knives. That was all."

Sylvie was confused. "But why did you marry him?"

"My own father had died. My mother was dying. We had no money. I had to leave the opera ballet." Yvette's face crumbled again. "I had to leave the ballet to marry a butcher." She pulled herself up straight. "But when he died, I swore that I would never again wash a butcher's bloodstained clothes. I was very lucky to have found Madame Hertier, a fine *bourgeoise* widow, a lovely woman who liked her lace rinsed in vinegar and her collars starched. And then Monsieur Moiret." She looked around rather desperately. "And now look! They are dead and the opera house is closed!"

Sylvie felt terrible, but with a quick glance she knew her mother felt worse. The masklike face began to crumble. Her mother was crushed.

"Mama!" Sylvie tugged on her hand. "We should go, Mama." They began to walk away and, as they did, Yvette looked back over her shoulder.

"It will open again, Sylvie. Believe me, it will. The world needs ballet. Not war. I cannot believe it. Complete nonsense!"

Sylvie shook her head. She was no longer sure what was nonsense and what wasn't. Did her mother's life make any sense? And was she her mother's daughter or just a dream child in ballet slippers and a *tutu*? Is this why Chantal became a dancer at Les Jolies Gamines instead of at the Paris Opera Ballet? Had she grown tired of being a dream child? Everything suddenly seemed unreal.

PART TWO

PARIS 1870
Autumn

Chapter 7

Her mother was right. The opera had reopened. *The world needs ballet,* Sylvie thought as she stood in the pitch-blackness of the stage.

The curtain was raised. There was a hush throughout the theater. A beam of limelight was focused on her. From the depths of the stage, however, in her white *tutu,* Sylvie knew she looked like no more than the tiniest pinprick of light. Behind her, in ascending order of height, were the other *petits rats,* and then the ranks of the company dancers, beginning with the members of the *quadrille,* then the *coryphée*s, followed by the *sujets,* or soloists. Next came the *premières danseuses,* or first soloists, and then the *danseuses étoile*s, or the prima ballerinas. So Sylvie, as the tiniest, at four feet eleven and one-quarter inch, was first in this great march, as it was called. The march was performed on every opening night of the fall and winter season of the Paris Opera Ballet.

Yes, Yvette Bertrand had been right that the world did need ballet. But it also seemed to have a deep lust for war. Yet there was no doubt that the French were much better at art than war. Against all expectations, several southern German states, independent of Prussia, had joined the war on the Prussian side. Somehow, the French intelligence had not known of the many secret treaties that existed between these states and the Prussians. Between the end of July and the end of August, the French troops had been defeated in a string of battles. But despite all, the ballet season still opened on September 2.

The program was to be simple because there had been precious little time to rehearse. Sylvie herself had barely seen her *petite mère*, Léontine Beaugrand, whose presence had been scarce around the school. She had had only one private session with her. But like a miser counting and recounting her gold, she had treasured this hour with Mademoiselle Léontine.

Over and over again she went through the smallest bits and pieces of her lesson. They ran through her head now.

"You are small," Mademoiselle Léontine had said. "But that means nothing. You must dance big. Your jumps must be higher, your arms bigger, your *pliés* deeper. . . . Never wait, Sylvie. You should not save anything. Dancing is now. Each step is precious."

And the step that Mademoiselle Léontine had wanted was one of the hardest dance steps of all, a *tour jeté*. It was a leaping turn with a scissorlike movement in which the front leg and the back leg switch positions during the midair rotation. One was supposed to land in an *arabesque*. It was the closest one could get to doing splits in the air while turning.

Sylvie's *tours jetés* had been quite sloppy that summer morning. So Mademoiselle Léontine, as she often did, asked Sylvie to close her eyes and visualize the step without moving.

"Now, Sylvie," she said in a very calm voice. "Imagine yourself about to do a *chassé*. You are going to keep your shoulders to the back corner of the *foyer*. You are looking at your front arm, which is extended. Keep looking until the last possible moment and then kick your front leg up, bring your arms up . . . turn, switch legs, and kick your back leg high, very high — yes." She slapped her hands together in a slicing motion. "Slice the air. Now, when you open your eyes you are going to do a perfect *tour jeté*."

And Sylvie had. As she landed perfectly, a sense of triumph swelled within her. Blissful triumph.

But now she must put that feeling away. She must concentrate on the performance she was in. As the music started, Mademoiselle Léontine's most important words streamed through Sylvie's mind:

"You must become the music and the music you, Sylvie." Then Léontine had quoted the great composer Berlioz. *"'Love can give no idea of music; music can give an idea of love. Why separate them? They are two wings of the same soul.' Music, Sylvie, is the soul of dance. You must convey that soul, that love."*

[61]

Yes, love, not war, Sylvie thought as she stepped through the blackness of the stage toward the audience.

Of course, the performance was over much too fast. She was once more stage furniture in an excerpt from *La Sylphide,* for which she received the extra twenty *sous.* But it was still thrilling, for Giuseppina had danced the role of La Sylphide, the fanciful creature who was half girl, half bird. Her costume was beautiful, with feathered wings and sprinkles of gold in her hair. She seemed like a gorgeous bejeweled bird of the night. Sylvie had watched her once more, and the steps were magnificent. Again she marveled at what a daring dancer Giuseppina was. What overwhelmed Sylvie the most was the way in which she dared balance. Her *arabesques,* her *pirouettes,* her *fouettés* were distillations of symmetry, masterpieces of equilibrium. She managed in some manner to push balance to the outer limits and then to suspend time in motion. It was breathtaking. *What a daredevil she is!* Sylvie thought.

She was very disappointed when, after the performance, Giuseppina rushed off. Sylvie had wanted to talk to her again, to tell her how wonderfully she had danced.

"Mama, she could have had four more curtain calls, I just know it!" Sylvie complained as they walked out of the alley behind the opera house and into the cool September night.

From the corner of her eye, Sylvie caught a glimpse of a shimmer, a golden flickering. Sylvie's breath locked in her throat. She clenched her mother's hand tightly. Two shadows hovered together on the street. One had a broom. One still had the traces of golden sprinkles in her hair.

"What is it, Sylvie?" Yvette asked. They had stopped walking.

Sylvie clamped her eyes shut for a second. "Nothing, Mama, nothing at all."

But what Sylvie had seen was deeply disturbing. It had been the street sweeper, the very same one they had seen on that summer morning when they had found the opera house closed. Sylvie had recognized him from the way he was leaning on his broom, and she had seen his face, which was cast in the demonic glow of his cigarette. But worst of all, he had been talking with Giuseppina. What could they have possibly been talking about—the dreamless man and the ballerina who was a dream? Luckily, Syvie's mother had been looking the other way and Sylvie quickly began to hurry along. "Let's turn here," she had said to her mother. "It's a lovely night. I always like to pass that flower shop on the corner."

But even as she turned, Sylvie had the strange sensation that the street sweeper was watching them. She tried to push him out of her mind by thinking about what Léontine had told her. The words of her *petite mère* came back to her as if through an eerie warp. *Steps are the words of dance. Steps are the language of ballet.*

But he knows nothing of such language, Sylvie thought. A shiver ran up her spine. Why was he talking to Giuseppina? What could he possibly have to do with her? Was there some reason that Giuseppina needed the strange man with his strange way of speaking? Sylvie felt the first tendrils of dread take root deep inside her. She was worried.

Chapter 8

Sylvie slept fitfully that night. In her dreams she kept seeing the image of the street sweeper, locked in the shadows with Giuseppina and then turning to look at her with his eerie green eyes. In the morning, Sylvie awoke to a different world. The French had suffered a calamitous defeat in a battle, and Napoléon III had been taken prisoner with one hundred thousand of his soldiers. The opera house was closed.

Two days later, on September 4, there was a bloodless revolution in Paris, and the Second French Empire came to an end. The government of the Third Republic had begun. The name most often heard on the streets was that of Léon Gambetta, the great orator and leader of the new government.

The crisp, cool weather of early September gave way to a stifling heat. The apartment became unbearable. Sylvie helped her mother with the washing in the courtyard behind their building. There was nothing else to do, really, since the opera house was closed.

The days were hot and formless. The hours passed slowly. Sylvie and her mother rarely left the apartment building. For the Bertrands, there were really only two realities—the one in the courtyard, strung with corridors of laundry, and the second reality of the shuttered opera house. The one spindly "tree" that crouched in a pot in a corner of the courtyard made Sylvie long for the magnificent trees the carpenters had built for the forest where the Wilis had danced in *Giselle*. And what, Sylvie wondered, was Monsieur Degas doing right now? Were the little rats dancing in his mind's eye? Was he perhaps painting at this very moment a ballerina unfolding her leg in a *developpé*?

The sun was harsh and of course there was no music, just the voices of people from the back alleys and streets, all telling bad news. There had been one defeat after another as the Prussians, now joined by the southern German states, moved with inexorable steadiness toward Paris. When Yvette Bertrand went out to collect laundry, she did not allow Sylvie to accompany her. "Only music should pour into your ears," she said. "Only music and the words of the ballet teachers."

Using a broomstick, she had fixed a *barre* of sorts for Sylvie and insisted that she practice her exercises every day. She would try to hum the music that was used in class, but Yvette herself had no real ear for music and hummed badly. Sylvie, however, kept the notes in her mind, could mark the counts, and moved through the *pliés*, the *tendus*, as if there were a small violin playing in her head. Her mother insisted that she wear her class *tutu*, the bow of the sash tied with the regulation tails no shorter than eight inches, no longer than ten.

And one morning, just as the first notes of a Brahms piece floated into Sylvie's mind, perfect for the deep *pliés* that began each class, Chantal swirled through the door.

"*Mon Dieu!* I don't believe it! What in heaven's name do you two think you are doing?"

"Practicing. We must continue," Yvette Bertrand replied curtly. "Just because there is all this nonsense going on does not mean life should stop."

"This," Chantal said, gesturing toward Sylvie at the broomstick *barre*, "is not life, Mama. This is foolishness."

"You know nothing. This is art."

"I know that the Prussians are not more than twenty miles from Paris. I know that in another few days Paris will be surrounded. I know that ballet, that 'art,' is not going to save you." She paused and smiled slyly. "Indeed, my art is going to attract a lot more soldiers than your art, Sylvie."

"That is not art!" Yvette exploded. Her face turned as red as if she were hanging over one of her laundry tubs of steaming suds. "That is shamelessness."

Chantal snorted. "Well, how would you like to make some money off my shamelessness?" She plunked a large bundle down on the table.

"What are you talking about?"

"The girls at the dance hall. They need their tights washed. They need a laundress at Les Jolies Gamines."

"Never!" Now the color drained from Yvette's face. She stared at the bundle as if it were some filthy, contaminated object. *As if*, Sylvie thought, *they were butchers' aprons.*

"Suit yourself." Chantal sniffed, and picked up the bundle. "But let me tell you, when the Prussians arrive, things are going to change. It is not going to be so easy to get food, and you will have to pay dearly for everything. So you might want to consider doing the shameless laundry of dance hall girls."

Yvette pressed her lips into a firm line and said nothing.

Sylvie looked from her mother to her sister and back. She suddenly felt stupid standing there in her perfectly starched *tutu*. She had even worn a black velvet ribbon around her throat like the girls in the company often did.

Chantal looked straight at that ribbon now. "Ah, you are a *sujet*? Or just a *coryphée*? I don't think the girls in the *quadrille* wear such ribbons."

Sylvie thought again of Giuseppina's thin little hand. What would happen if Chantal was right, if it was hard to get food? Giuseppina could not get any skinnier than she already was. Would Sylvie's own hands begin to feel like chicken bones? She stole a look at her mother. *Maybe Mama should give in to Chantal, just this once, and do the laundry.* But she could tell by the set of her mother's mouth this was not going to happen. There would be no giving in.

When Chantal left and shut the door behind her, Yvette

turned to Sylvie and attempted to resume humming the Brahms piece. But Sylvie stepped away from the broomstick.

"Mama, should we be scared?"

"Of course not. She knows nothing."

"But, Mama, everyone says that they are coming. The Prussians, the Germans. Will we starve?"

"No, we will not starve. Don't be ridiculous. This will all blow over. The opera house will open again. So you must be prepared. Now back to your *barre*. Quick! Quick!" Yvette flicked her hand as if she were shooing a fly away.

"Yes, Mama." *This is so stupid*, Sylvie thought. *Mama, when will you wake up from your dream? Your dream could get us killed!*

It was not a quarter of an hour later that a thunderous roar rolled through the small apartment and seemed to shake the entire building. This was followed by a sizzling crack.

"The Prussians!" Sylvie cried.

"Nonsense, it's a thunderstorm. Quick, we have to get the laundry in before it is all drenched!" Yvette cried out.

Sylvie and her mother flew down the stairs to the courtyard. By the time they got there the rain was coming down in sheets and the wind was lashing through the laundry. The entire courtyard looked like a ship foundering at sea, with its sails flailing in a gale.

"Get the lacework first!" Yvette screamed above the roar of the thundershower. Lightning flashed, cracking open the sky, peeling back the skin of the purple twilight.

[69]

It didn't take them long to gather in the laundry, but by the time they returned to their apartment, they were both soaked. Sylvie caught a glimpse of herself in the mirror she used when she practiced. The drenched white tulle of her *tutu* hung like dead birds from her small body. Her black hair was plastered to her head.

"Just look at your *tutu*!" Yvette sighed.

Mama, Sylvie wanted to say. *Does it matter? Does it really matter? They say the Prussians are twenty miles away, or less. What are we going to do? Dance our way through this war?*

"Well. Let's get this hung up." Yvette went to a cupboard and fetched the ball of cord she used for stringing clothes to dry inside. Soon it was the apartment that looked like a ship of laundry sailing on a windless sea. But at least the thunderstorm had broken the fearsome heat.

Sylvie and her mother went to bed exhausted. The sound of the occasional drips of the drying clothes was magnified in Sylvie's head to the thump of soldiers' feet marching toward Paris. Closer and closer they came—fifteen miles, then ten, then eight, six, two . . .

Are they here, Mama? she whispered in her dream. *Are they here yet?*

And, in her dream, her mother answered, *Nonsense. One more* plié, *now the* pas de bourrée, *fast, fast, travel, Sylvie, move, you can float away from them on your toes,* chérie.

Chapter 9

The very next day, on September 19, the Germans and the Prussians encircled Paris and the grueling siege had begun. On that same day, Yvette returned from delivering laundry, absolutely giddy. As if in defiance of the siege, the school for the Paris Opera Ballet had reopened. *Perhaps we can dance our way through this war,* Sylvie thought.

"Hurry! Hurry! There is to be class at eleven. Fetch your things."

"But, Mama, that *tutu* is a mess."

"Don't worry. These are extreme times."

This was the only concession that Yvette made that there was a war going on—a war that had slightly inconvenienced the world of dance. She had acknowledged that one reality had grazed another.

An hour later, as Sylvie and her mother turned into the Rue le Peletier, Yvette stopped suddenly. Sylvie immediately caught sight of what had arrested her mother's insistent trot toward the opera house. It was the street sweeper. Yvette glared at him as if to say, *See, you lout! You filthy* communard, *on the very day the Germans come we will dance!* They continued up the steps to the opera house, Yvette firmly gripping Sylvie's hand.

From the moment they stepped through the door, Sylvie knew that her mother was right. She felt all the tension of the last few weeks melt away. The familiar smells of the grand old place greeted her like long-lost friends as she made her way through the corridors to the *foyer de la danse*: the dry, pungent scent of the carpentry shop; the slightly musty odor of the costume department; the paint of the scenery workshop.

She peeked into the open door. The room was empty, but there was a flat tree propped up in its full autumnal glory. Its leaves were made of a wonderful new fabric called *tissu d'Egypte* that could be used in both costumes and scenery. And there was the moon from *Giselle* and the storefront from the doll shop of *Coppélia*. This, of course, made Sylvie think of Giuseppina Bozzacchi. She could not wait to see her again. Since classes had resumed, the advanced classes of Madame Venozzi would certainly be in session. There had been plans to once more present *Coppélia* in the fall/winter season. The audiences were mad for it and for the little Italian *danseuse étoile*.

But Giuseppina was not there. Nor was she there the next day or the following one. The girl seemed to have vanished into thin air. Nobody seemed to know where she had gone. It was the talk of the opera house. Indeed, Sylvie realized that she might have been the very last person to have seen Giuseppina, on that street corner after the performance of *La Sylphide*.

Sylvie could not help but think of the street sweeper. Would *he* know where the tiny ballerina had gone? Sylvie was still haunted by the sight of Giuseppina conversing with him. It was as if the sprinkles of gold dust in Giuseppina's hair streamed through Sylvie's dreams. Upon waking in the morning, she had the sensation that she might have dreamed of Giuseppina, but the dream then seemed to flit away, much like the chimerical creature the Italian had danced in the ballet.

And every time Sylvie awoke from this dream, there was a terrible foreboding, a presentiment that something awful was just waiting to happen. She would often clutch her own hands and then remember how Giuseppina's had felt so thin when she had shaken it. She wondered if she would ever have the nerve to ask the street sweeper if he knew where the ballerina lived.

Much to Sylvie and her mother's distress, Sylvie's *petite mère* was also gone. *Her* disappearance was not a mystery.

"She's what?" Yvette Bertrand gasped.

"Yes, madame, she is involved in the war effort," Jeanne Mercier, one of the assistant teachers, said to Sylvie and her mother after class one day.

"War effort?" Yvette repeated blankly.

"Yes, madame. You know, to help the many wounded soldiers who have been arriving daily." No one could get out of Paris and no supplies could get in, but the wounded had streamed into the city just two days before the siege began.

"She has been organizing a soldiers' hospital at the Comédie-Française."

"The Comédie-Française," Yvette moved her mouth around the two words as if she had never spoken them before. "But that is a theater—for Molière." Her face crumpled into a look of profound disappointment.

"I know, madame, but so it goes."

"So it goes?" Yvette blinked in dismay.

"And Mademoiselle Léontine is also organizing groups to collect food. For the anticipated shortages."

"Groups!" Yvette Bertrand was now genuinely horrified. "She is not a *communard*, I hope!"

Sylvie knew in that moment exactly what was going through her mother's mind. If Léontine Beaugrand was a *communard* or the member of any "group," she had no business being the *petite mère* of her precious daughter. Ballerinas were not beasts. They could not be herded into "groups." Ballerinas did not organize anything.

Sylvie herself was experiencing an entirely different range of emotions. She was stunned, yes, but not for exactly the same reasons. She could not say that she was actually disappointed. More than anything, she was curious. Extremely curious. And the Comédie-Française was only a few blocks away. Her mother, however, would never let her go there. But why did her mother have to know? In the afternoons, Yvette usually made her rounds to collect the laundry from her clients. And there were precious few. Sylvie's mother had planned to go visit some other potential households in the fancy neighborhoods that her clients had recommended. There was actually a countess on the Rue du Faubourg Saint-Honoré whom she had great hopes for. If indeed she went that afternoon, it would give Sylvie time to break away between classes.

And there was one other thing: Sylvie planned to find Giuseppina.

"Well . . . well . . . well." That was all Sylvie's mother could say as she watched Jeanne Mercier walk away. Yvette Bertrand straightened herself a bit. "Notice, Sylvie, how Mademoiselle Mercier walks. She has a lovely turnout, doesn't she? I understand that she is quite a good teacher, although I have never observed her teaching. But I do hear that she is quite wonderful in that *pas de deux* in *La Sylphide*. And I have heard rumors that she is soon to be promoted from *sujet* to *première danseuse*. And then to *danseuse étoile!*"

Sylvie's suspicions were confirmed. A new *petite mère*! But nonetheless Sylvie was perfectly happy with Mademoiselle Léontine, even if she was not here. For Sylvie, Léontine Beaugrand had suddenly become an object of mystery, something larger than she had ever imagined, larger than life. Yes, had not her *petite mère* told her to dance big even though she was small? The words came back to her:

You must dance big . . . your jumps must be higher, your arms bigger, your pliés *deeper. . . . Well,* Sylvie thought, *Mademoiselle Léontine was living big.* And suddenly, Sylvie had an urge she could not deny.

[75]

She, too, wanted to live big. She wanted to explore that world outside the opera house. Outside the scents of sawdust and pasteboard, paint and rosin. She had a sudden inspiration. She turned to her mother. "Mama, wasn't Mercier the name of the new client you were going to see about this afternoon?"

"Why, yes, Sylvie. What a coincidence!"

"Madame Henri Mercier, 8 Rue du Faubourg Saint-Honoré." Sylvie smiled brightly at her mother. Her eyes twinkled. Yvette's face was suddenly animated. "Why, I think this is a sign, Sylvie, a good omen. I must go at once, this afternoon."

"Yes, Mama, I think so. And I will dance better if I know you have a chance of getting some new clients."

"Now, Sylvie. I don't want you to worry."

"That's just the point, Mama. I will *not* worry if I know you have a special new client like Madame Mercier."

"Oh, my little Sylvie! You will be *une danseuse étoile*. I just know it." She held Sylvie's small chin in her hand, tipped it up as if examining a fine piece of china, and then kissed her on each cheek.

Chapter 10

Sylvie turned at the southwest corner of the Palais-Royal and entered the Place du Palais-Royal. Directly ahead were the immense pillars of the Comédie-Française. She walked past a bust of Molière in the courtyard and hurried up the steps to the big main entrance. The doors seemed to be shut. She would have to look for a stage door. Sylvie had a natural instinct for where stage doors might be.

She turned and walked in the opposite direction from which she had come and rounded a corner of the building. Her instincts had not failed her. People were bustling in and out of a wide door. There were men limping on crutches with the help of a friend or family member and there were others being carried in on stretchers. She walked quickly toward the bustle and soon found herself behind a man with a bandaged head. On either side of him were two nuns supporting him as he attempted to walk.

Horrific smells began to assault Sylvie almost at once, and they became more intense as she entered the theater. She found herself in a backstage area that was filled wall-to-wall with cots of moaning, bleeding men. She blinked as she saw another nun, wearing the tiny spectacles called *pince-nez*, or nose pinchers, lean over a man who was a ghastly green color. The nun put her head very close to his chest while holding his wrist. Suddenly, she dropped his wrist and made the sign of the cross, her lips mumbling an inaudible prayer. She then snapped a dirty sheet over his face. "*Un autre mort ici!*"

He's dead! Sylvie whispered to herself. *I just saw a man die!*

She turned to leave. Directly in front of her was a man on a cot, moaning. When she looked down, she saw that his leg ended in a bloodied, bandaged stump at his ankle. She felt a wave of nausea swim up inside her. She squeezed her eyes shut, closed her mouth, and swallowed. The stage had begun to swirl slowly. She swayed.

"Sylvie!" A voice called out to her and she felt someone grab her arm.

"Mademoiselle Léontine!" Sylvia opened her eyes.

"We do not have time for silly little girls, Mademoiselle Léontine. One of your ballerinas, eh?" It was the nun with the nose-pinching spectacles.

Quickly, her *petite mère* began pulling her across the stage — across this stage smeared with blood and vomit — no limelights, no silvery moons. But Mademoiselle Léontine was transporting her so swiftly it felt as if she were streaking across the floor in a string of bloodstained *bourrées* that were part of some gruesome *pas de deux*.

Mademoiselle Léontine sat her down on a stool. "Sylvie, dear child. What are you doing here?"

Sylvie looked around. Her dark eyes were wide and fearful. Léontine Beaugrand reached out her hand and gently touched Sylvie's cheek. "This is no place for you."

"I know, but . . ."

"But what, my dear?"

"But I do not belong at the ballet, either." She looked around. "At least not now." Then she looked down at her feet, as if trying to imagine the pink satin ballet slippers.

Mademoiselle Léontine leaned forward. "Look at me, Sylvie." Sylvie looked up. "What are you saying? What do you mean, you do not belong in the ballet?" Mademoiselle Léontine waited.

Sylvie was not sure how to answer the question. At this moment, she felt completely confused. She felt she was caught between two worlds: one of paint and magic, of tulle and ballet slippers; the other of blood and suffering, bandages and footless men. It was too shocking, too overwhelming.

"I see all this," Sylvie began to speak in a frail whisper. "And suddenly to be standing at a *barre* and raising my arms in a *port de bras* when I see right there a man with no arm . . ." She nodded toward the middle of the stage. "It makes no sense." Her mother was always saying certain things were nonsense, but the whole world made no sense now, none whatsoever. "It is insane to be dancing now!" she blurted out. "*You* are not there, mademoiselle. You see that, don't you? How crazy it is? *C'est fou! Complètement fou!*"

Mademoiselle Léontine bit lightly on her lower lip. Her eyes filled with tears, and she cupped the side of her face with her hand. Sylvie saw the dismay in her face. She could hardly believe what she had just said. Somewhere deep within, Sylvie felt herself grow old — very, very old. "Sylvie," Léontine finally said, "I do understand what you are saying. But still this is no place for you."

Sylvie swallowed. She knew that Mademoiselle Léontine was right. Everything sickened her here. But how could she go back to ballet class now? The thought of raising her leg in an *arabesque* or tying the ribbons of her ballet slippers sickened her, too. Her mouth began to tremble as if she were about to cry. *I cannot cry. I simply cannot cry!*

"Sylvie, if you want to help, not here, but elsewhere, you can."

Sylvie looked up brightly for the first time. "How? What can I do?" Suddenly, the flecks sparkled and Sylvie's eyes seemed to glow with tiny golden galaxies of light.

"We need to collect food. The shortages have already started. Can you read or write at all?"

"A little bit."

The little rats barely had any education outside the *foyer de la danse.* Many of them were completely illiterate. Sylvie knew that Léontine Beaugrand knew this as well. "Well, that is good and maybe you will learn a little bit more. You see, I have lists of people, rich people and merchants, who have agreed to donate food from their stores. Many have homes with farms in the countryside. We need volunteers to go around to these people and ask what they can give and when we might collect it. And, if the goods are coming from the countryside, which break in the blockade of the city they will come through."

"Breaks?"

"Yes, we have organized breaks in the blockade. They have code names that our donors are familiar with. So would you like to help in this way?"

"Oh, yes, mademoiselle. Yes!"

"What would your mother say?"

Sylvie took a split second to reflect. "I think she would approve," Sylvie lied. "Yes, I am sure." She nodded quickly, then looked down at her feet.

She knows I'm lying, Sylvie thought. Then Léontine Beaugrand sighed. "All right. You live in Le Marais, is that not so?"

"Yes, mademoiselle, near the Place des Vosges."

"Good. I will try to compose a list for your neighborhood."

Good, Sylvie thought. Her mother often sent her out on small errands and she could make excuses to leave the house. But there was one problem. That was on the weekend days when there was no afternoon class. Her mother accompanied her every day to class and often sat in class. Would it not be easier if Sylvie could have a list that was closer to the opera house neighborhood?

"But, Mademoiselle Léontine, my mother often does laundry for very rich families near the opera house. Perhaps it would be good if I also had a list for this neighborhood as well," Sylvie suggested.

Léontine Beaugrand raised one eyebrow, her face displaying a fleeting skepticism. "Yes, of course. Very good. I will get that list for you, too."

Chapter 11

It was the fourth day that Sylvie had been "running the lists," as it was called, for the food collection groups. When she stepped out of the opera house that afternoon, she once more felt the thrill, a thrill she had never anticipated, of leaving an unreal world behind. The real trees seemed to breathe, and the waters of the Seine sparkled despite the refuse. The pasteboard trees and painted seas seemed somehow wrong. She did not miss the fantasy she had left behind. The real question was how had she not missed the real world that she was now encountering.

When she would meet Mademoiselle Léontine at the makeshift hospital of the Comédie-Française to receive her lists, the terrible smells still assaulted her and the sight of the maimed soldiers was almost unbearable. But she bore it. Someway. Somehow. She did not feel especially proud for enduring this new reality, with its appalling sights, but in some unexplainable way she felt more alive than she ever had before, even though she was now often hungry.

Yes, the pinch had finally come. Everything was hard to get and prices had soared. Bakeries all over Paris had closed. There was no more fresh produce; only dried meat and salted dried fish could be purchased. Luckily for Sylvie, Countess Mercier sometimes sent some bread and cheese home with Yvette. The countess herself was on the collection lists of Léontine Beaugrand. When Sylvie had mentioned that her mother worked for the countess, Mademoiselle Léontine was careful not to put her on Sylvie's list.

But now there was a new problem. It had been announced that very day that the opera house was to be closed once more because of the siege. It was not only that the students, the members of the company, and the teachers were too hungry to dance. The weather was turning cold and too many of the thousands of people who made the great fantasy factory run were being called up to help out in other places. It would become too expensive to keep the coal furnaces and boilers running to heat the *foyer de la danse*.

Sylvie was going to have to come up with some excuse to get out of their apartment. Luckily, the countess Mercier had asked Yvette if she might do the laundry at her home on the Rue du Faubourg Saint-Honoré since her own laundress had had to leave to nurse a wounded son back from the front. But this only took care of three afternoons a week. Sylvie would have to think of something for the other days.

In the meantime, she had another, more pressing, concern on her mind. Giuseppina. There still had been no sign of the

Italian ballerina for months and Sylvie had no time to look for her. But today she planned to begin, even if she would be late getting to the Comédie-Française. First, she had to go to look for the lost ballerina in the place she had last seen her. There were many shops in that region, and although their cupboards were nearly bare, she was sure that Giuseppina must have shopped in them at one time. Maybe she could ask some of the storekeepers for information.

An hour later, Sylvie had gone into every shop on the Rues Richer and Drouot. Of course many were closed, but not one of the available shopkeepers had seen the tiny Italian ballerina. "*Non*, mademoiselle, no one by that description. You say she is a famous dancer?" Sylvie nodded. "Well, these are difficult times. Maybe she somehow got out of Paris and back to Italy. Smart move, I would say."

"Yes, yes," Sylvie replied, and her stomach seemed to rumble in agreement. She was so hungry. She hoped that her mother might bring home some bread and cheese from the countess's estates in Normandy.

Sylvie had to give up her search that day and report back to the Comédie-Française for her list. She looked over her shoulder as she walked. Whenever Léontine handed her the list, she would deliver a sober warning about black marketers. There was a thriving black market for food, and it was key that these people not get hold of the lists that identified the donors or collection points. Sylvie always had to make sure she was not being followed. Also, she knew there were spies who would like to crack the code of where the breaks in the blockade were.

"Sylvie! Sylvie!" a voice called from behind her as she turned the corner to head for the Comédie-Française. It was her friend Isabel.

"You always disappear," Isabel said. "We have not had lunch together for a long time. Did you only like me when I brought you cheese from the shop where my mother works?"

"Oh, no, Isabel! That is not true at all. But doesn't your mother still get cheese?"

"No. They closed the shop."

"Oh, dear."

"Well, now she has a job as a doorkeeper on the Rue Jean-Jacques Rousseau. But why have you missed all the afternoon classes? Not that it matters anymore."

Sylvie did not quite know what to say. She hated the thought of lying to her friend. But then a sudden idea burst into her mind. "Isabel, what are you going to do now that there is no ballet class?"

Isabel shrugged. "Not much. Be bored. What are you going to do?"

"Isabel, can you keep a secret?"

"Of course. What is it? I knew you were up to something, Sylvie Bertrand. I just knew it!"

So Sylvie explained about Léontine Beaugrand and what she had been doing to help for the last four days. "But my mother would have a fit if she knew what I was doing. Would yours?"

"No, my mother doesn't care a bit. All she cares about now is the new boyfriend she has. He is the one who got her the job as the doorkeeper."

"Good. Because here is my idea. You can help me run the lists. But now that the school is closed I must make up a lie for my mother."

"What lie?" Isabel looked at her narrowly with her icy blue-gray eyes. Isabel was as fair as Sylvie was dark.

"I will tell my mother that I am going to your apartment to practice. That we want to be ready when the ballet school opens again. She will love the idea."

Isabel positively glowed. Her life, Sylvie knew, was a lonely one. Her older sister had left Paris and married someone in Provence. She had a brother, but now he was away, fighting in this war. Her mother was one of the few mothers who didn't care one way or the other if her daughter made it into the company of the Paris Opera Ballet. She was often away from the apartment she shared with Isabel for several days at a time. She never bothered to tell her daughter where she went but usually left a little money for her to buy food. Sometimes when Isabel came home after class, she would find a modest dinner set out for her. A piece of cheese, usually, and a bowl of milk.

Isabel had once told Sylvie that she often thought of herself as more of a pet than a daughter. "A cat," she had said.

"Why a cat?" Sylvie had asked.

"She pets me, my mother. She loves my hair. When she comes home, especially after being away for a few days, she always wants me to lie with my head in her lap and she runs her fingers through my hair."

"Well, you do have lovely hair," Sylvie had replied. It was the truth; Isabel had thick, silky blond hair. It was all Sylvie could think to say. It seemed very odd to her.

The life of a cat-child must be very lonely, and Sylvie knew that was what Isabel liked most about the opera house — she was never alone when she was there. She even enjoyed the scoldings from Madame Théodore, because it meant someone was really looking at her, paying attention to her, and not simply running her fingers through her hair.

When the director announced that morning, in the *foyer de la danse*, that this would be the last class and that the opera house would be closed indefinitely, Sylvie had watched as Isabel's face turned gray. What, she wondered, would poor Isabel do? With her mother always gone, her life would be as empty as her belly. The days would loom large and endless. Sylvie had to admit that, as annoying as her own mother often was, as frustrated as Sylvie often became with being her mother's dream, Yvette was there. Some people were hungry for food, but Isabel was starving for company, for friendship. Sylvie had worried that the loneliness of the days ahead would truly crush Isabel. But now all that had changed. Isabel's eyes sparkled as she grabbed Sylvie's hand.

"Oh, Sylvie! That is so wonderful. I will help you as best I can," she cried.

"But I have to warn you about the hospital where we must pick up the lists. It is awful—terrible smells and bad things. Lots of blood and men missing arms and legs. Usually, Mademoiselle Léontine comes out the stage door and meets me, so I do not have to go in, but sometimes I do have to go in and find her."

Isabel squared her narrow shoulders. "I will be fine. Don't worry."

"And there is one more thing that is very important."

"What is that?"

Sylvie's eyes grew darker. The golden flecks dimmed. "You know how Giuseppina has disappeared?"

"Yes, it is a mystery."

"It is a mystery I plan to solve." There was heat in Sylvie's voice when she spoke.

Isabel looked at Sylvie in awe. "Sylvie," she began. "Until now I thought you were just like all the other little rats. I mean, you are my best friend. But still, I just thought . . . well, you know how it is . . . that mostly you just wanted to scuttle up to the advanced classes, be chosen for the company, and then join the *quadrille* and hope for the *coryphée* and then *sujet* and so on. But you are really different, Sylvie."

Sylvie felt herself blush and looked down.

"No, you really are! You have imagination for much more than scuttling up some stupid ladder."

"It's not that stupid," Sylvie protested.

"Maybe not, Sylvie, but you see much more than if you were at the top of that ladder. You see a whole different world!"

That very afternoon, the two girls began working on the lists, and the next morning they would meet again to start their search for Giuseppina.

Chapter 12

Sylvie and Isabel had just parted ways after working on their lists. As she often did on her way home, Sylvie stopped on the bridge to look at the water flowing beneath it — the real water of this newly discovered real world. She was so mesmerized by the flowing river that she did not realize someone had walked up beside her and was also leaning on the bridge.

"It is very pretty in its own way, despite the garbage, isn't it?"

"Chantal!" Sylvie exclaimed. "What are you doing here?"

"Maybe I should ask the same of you."

Sylvie would never know why she blurted out what she said next. It was as if the question had been festering in her for years.

"Chantal," Sylvie burst out. "Why did you leave the ballet?"

"Well, you know why. Hasn't Mama said it enough times? I was a lazy fool."

Sylvie looked at her sister carefully. "No, I mean really," she said.

"Really?" Chantal gave a sharp little laugh. "You mean you don't believe Mama?"

"Not always."

Chantal lifted one eyebrow quizzically. "Ah, little one, are you starting to have doubts? My! My!"

"Don't call me 'little one,'" Sylvie shot back. "I know more than you think."

"And just what do you know?" Chantal challenged.

Sylvie looked her straight in the eyes. "I know that it wasn't just laziness. I know that you wanted to be something more than just Mama's dream."

Chantal's face softened. There was an expression of near disbelief in her eyes. "Sylvie, you know this? How do you know?"

"I just do."

Chantal leaned on the bridge and looked down into the water again. "You were just an infant when Papa died. But I wasn't. They argued all the time. Papa hated the ballet. But when he died, Mama felt there was no obstacle now to my being part of the ballet. At first, I liked it—no more arguments. But then I saw that Mama was living her life through me."

"You were her dream child," Sylvie whispered to the gray water beneath them.

"Yes, I suppose you could say that. But I didn't want to be a dream. There was a girl who lived nearby, Catherine. She went to school. She had friends whom she did not have to compete with all the time. I hated that in the ballet, the way the girls were always competing. It was as if you couldn't trust anybody. And the girls' mothers were worse, trying to impress the teachers."

"Like Madame du Bac."

"Oh, yes, definitely. I wanted real friends in the real world. I wanted to learn to read. I *was* learning, too. Catherine was teaching me, but then she moved away. I still tried to learn on my own, and I did."

"You know how to read, really read?"

"I read books—all the time. And newspapers, too. Mama wouldn't hear of me quitting, of course. So I . . . I"—Chantal shrugged her shoulders—"I guess I made up my mind that if I was lazy enough, sloppy enough, they would throw me out."

"And then you could have your own dreams?" Sylvie asked hesitantly.

Chantal sighed. "Oh, I'm not sure how well I've done with that. But at least they would be *my* dreams and not Mama's."

"But was dancing at Les Jolies Gamines part of your dream?"

"Of course not." Chantal snorted. "But I had to take what little I had and go with it, you know, try to make a living. Mama wouldn't have me at home if I wasn't in the Paris Opera Ballet school. I was almost fifteen. Old enough to live on my own. But I do more than just dance at Les Jolies Gamines."

"You do?"

Chantal nodded.

"What?"

"I am starting to find a new dream." She smiled and it was not a smug smile or the sneering one she often flashed when she was with Sylvie and Yvette.

"What is this dream? Can you tell me?" Sylvie asked.

"Not yet."

"Please, Chantal, please." Sylvie felt as if this was the first real conversation she had ever had with her sister. "Just a hint?"

"You won't understand it."

"Stop telling me I am too little and won't understand things." The exasperation in Sylvie's voice was clear.

"Well, if I told you I dream of a better world, would you understand?"

"What do you mean by a better world?" Sylvie asked.

"A fairer world, one where things are more equal."

"Things aren't fair?" Sylvie wondered aloud.

"Of course not, Sylvie. Is it fair that poor Mama has to slave away washing rich peoples' clothes for such miserable money?"

This was the first time Sylvie had ever heard a sympathetic word out of Chantal's mouth about their mother. And, for some reason, this talk of unfairness reawakened in Sylvie the feeling of dread she had been harboring about Giuseppina.

"Chantal, I must ask you something."

"What is it?" Chantal sensed the urgency in her sister's voice.

"The little Italian ballerina, Giuseppina Bozzacchi? She has disappeared. I know what you're thinking—one less Italian ballerina . . ."

"No, no," Chantal protested. "How hard-hearted do you think I am?"

Less, thought Sylvie, *less than I ever thought before.* But she kept these thoughts to herself. "I am worried about her, very worried. I have actually been trying to find her."

"You have?" Chantal's eyes opened wide.

"Yes," Sylvie nodded. "As you say, some things aren't fair. She might be dancing in all the lead roles, but she is too thin. I am so worried, and she doesn't speak French that well."

"The Italians hang about together. I'll ask around." Chantal paused. "You know some of them are *communards.*"

"They are?"

"Yes," Chantal replied with a distant look in her eyes.

"What are you thinking about, Chantal?"

"Everything. Everything that isn't fair in life. There is so much. You think about it, Sylvie. Is it fair that men and mere boys are forced to fight in a war not of their choosing? Is it even fair that only men are conscripted into the army, not women?"

"Women fighting?" Sylvie blinked in utter amazement. "You want to fight, Chantal?"

"For the right cause, I would fight to the death." Chantal's bright red curls quivered across her forehead. Her eyes were fierce and uncompromising as she looked at Sylvie.

"Really, Chantal?"

"Really, Sylvie."

"I . . . I . . ." Sylvie stammered. "I had better go now. Mama will worry if I am too late."

"Of course, Mama will worry . . ." Chantal's voice dwindled off. Something had been left unsaid as if she was either too lazy or too tired to finish the sentence. As Sylvie turned to walk the rest of the way across the bridge, she felt she was caught between two worlds, two dreams. *What is my dream?* she wondered. *Mine, my very own?*

Chapter 13

"Ah, Sylvie," Yvette Bertrand clapped her hands together. "How charming it is that you and dear little Isabel are practicing. You watch. When the opera reopens, you will be promoted to the advanced class, mark my words!"

This is the perfect lie! Sylvie thought.

But now her mother was saying, "Yes, I think maybe I should stop by today and watch you."

Oh, no! Sylvie thought fast. "Not today, Mama. Isabel and I are working on the Dolls' Duet from *Coppélia*."

"The Dolls' Duet?"

"Yes, it is a new one that Mérante and Saint-Léon were thinking about putting in the ballet this past summer."

Yvette Bertrand crossed herself and whispered, "Saint-Léon of blessed memory." Saint-Léon, who had written the story *Coppélia*, which was choreographed by Louis Mérante, had died just two weeks before.

Sylvie pushed the theme a bit. "We felt, Mama, it would be a fitting tribute to him, to try and practice the steps for this new part of the ballet that he loved so much."

"Ah, Sylvie, you are so sensitive."

Sort of, Sylvie thought. She had been genuinely sad when Monsieur Saint-Léon had died, but it was a total lie that he and Mérante had created something called the Dolls' Duet. Now Sylvie was going to have to think up one herself! Lies could get one into trouble.

"And just think," Yvette continued ecstatically. "When the opera reopens, you and Isabel will be ready to dance this duet. So when can I come and see it?" she asked eagerly.

Think quickly, mon Dieu! "Uh . . . well, I'll ask Isabel when she thinks she'll be ready. I mean, we have a lot more work to do on it."

Sylvie grabbed her toe shoes and her *tutu* and put them in the satchel. Slinging it over her shoulder, she kissed her mother good-bye. Her stomach growled loudly.

"Here, dear," her mother said. "I have another piece of bread and this bit of cheese. Take it with you."

"But, Mama, this is yours. I already ate mine."

"You are a growing girl and you are dancing now. You need it."

"But, Mama!" Sylvie looked at her mother with real alarm. They had both grown thinner in the past several days. But she now saw that the once soft contours of her mother's face looked almost sharp. "Mama, I can't!"

"Sylvie, listen to me."

"But, Mama, you're not going to the countess's today. She

always at least gives you coffee and a bit of something. You'll be hungry all day long."

Yvette Bertrand looked severely at her daughter and raised one finger, shaking it. "Sylvie, I am the mother. You are the daughter. You do as I say. I am a simple laundress, and you are a ballerina. You must eat! No more words. *Compris?*"

"Yes, Mama, I understand."

Sylvie felt awful. Guilt washed over her. She was taking food from her own mother's mouth. It was all part of a big lie and the lie was becoming more and more complicated. *Well,* she thought, *Isabel and I must truly work on this Dolls' Duet. We will have to come up with something.*

In May, Sylvie had been a toy in Dr. Coppelius's workshop in the first act. But neither she nor the other *petits rats* had been among the animated toys that got to come to life when Swanilda goes on her rampage. She could still, however, recall the music of that scene perfectly. It started light, very expressive of the character and the mood of the shop. But even as Swanilda's rampage grew and the tempo of the music quickened, it never overpowered the drama that was happening on the stage.

As she walked down the street, Sylvie began to sketch out the counts, her fingers dancing lightly against her skirt. When dancers did this, it was known as marking. It was a way of visualizing and writing the steps into one's memory without dancing full-out. One could do it very lightly with her fingers or her feet, unless her feet were hurrying along like Sylvie's, toward her meeting place with Isabel.

She rushed up to Isabel as soon as she spotted her. "Do you have a broomstick at your apartment?" she asked breathlessly.

"A broomstick? Yes, but why?"

Sylvie explained her idea.

"You mean we actually have to make up a duet?" Isabel cried.

"Not much, not much, don't worry. Only about five minutes."

"Five minutes is a lot. It takes a lot of steps to fill five minutes!"

"Well, say four. Look, I already have part of it figured out." Sylvie put down her satchel. "Here. Cross your arms and take my hands." Sylvie reached out with one hand. "No, no, wrong hand. Like this." The two girls crossed their arms in such a way that each was clasping the hands of the other as they faced forward. Each then turned out her left foot and placed it in front of her right. This was the classic preparatory position that allowed the dancer to effortlessly step out and begin any sequence without her shifting weight.

"Now what?" Isabel asked as a woman walked by, looked at them curiously, and then muttered something before going on.

"All right. This is the first combination. Follow me. Step out . . . *pas de bourrée* . . . *bourrée*." The girls rose onto the tiptoes of their shabby ankle-high boots. *"Pas de bourrée . . . bourrée . . . bourrée . . .* travel . . . travel . . . travel toward that streetlamp."* Sylvie was talking as she silently kept track of the counts in her head. A few more people stopped briefly to look at them. She heard an old man snort, "They're dancing and Paris is starving!"

"All right, now *piqué* to *arabesque.*" Each girl, trying to stay in unison, pointed her right foot and pricked the sidewalk lightly with her boot toes. "Now, *pas de bourrée!* Now, *chassé.*" The two girls slid together toward another streetlamp. Then *brisé . . . brisé.*" They both shot into the air and crossed their boots quickly back and forth before landing. "Now, two *pas de chat!*" With the cat jumps, they once more rose into the air but this time with their knees bent.

When they landed Sylvie said, *"Fini."*

"The end! But that was only twelve beats, the whole thing."

"The end of the first combination. Come on, enough dancing. We have to get the lists and then look for Giuseppina."

Chapter 14

Luckily, the lists were not too long that day. Sylvie and Isabel went up the stoop of a very grand-looking house on the Rue de Richelieu. Sylvie lifted the door knocker. They were to always go to the front door so a maid would not dismiss them from the service door as some poor children looking for food.

A maid in a white cap opened the door. She immediately frowned at the two little girls. *"Non! Non!"* She began shaking her finger. Sylvie had become an expert at this. She pulled from her pocket a thick cream-colored envelope that had an important-looking seal on it. It was the kind of envelope in which invitations or messages were delivered. The maid wrinkled her nose and looked at it, clearly pretending to read.

"It is for the count," Sylvie told her. "Kindly give it to him directly. We will wait."

Within two minutes, the maid came back with the envelope. Neatly folded inside would be the items that the count in question could provide, and when and where the pickup should be made.

There were only two more stops, and then they were done.

"I cannot spend too much time looking for Giuseppina today, Sylvie, I am sorry to say. My mother is coming back with a new friend to the apartment, and she insists I clean it." Isabel sighed.

"Don't worry. Tomorrow we will have most of the day."

"And what about the Dolls' Duet for *Coppélia?*"

"I'll think up another combination on my way home. You know we don't have to be perfect for Mama."

"Well, if you say so."

The next day, their hunt took them close to the construction of the new home for the Paris Opera—"the hole." They stopped by the wire fencing to peer through. "Look, they really have done a lot. All the walls are up," Sylvie said.

"Sylvie! See that man over there walking up and down?"

"Where?"

"There," said Isabel pointing. "The man in the tall silk hat. I am almost sure that is the architect Charles Garnier."

"Really? Have you seen him before?"

"Yes. When I was having my examination last time, and there was no place for me to take it except in the *petit foyer* with the slightly raked floor. It slants just a bit at one end, you know?" Sylvie nodded. "Well," Isabel continued. "He came into the *petit foyer* in the middle of my examination just to have a look at the floor."

The stages of theaters were raked, or slanted, at a slight angle to give the audience a better view. It took some getting used to, especially going "uphill"; you had to dance much harder. So the beginning performance classes were always taught in these *foyers*.

"So that is the same man?" Sylvie asked.

"Yes, I would recognize him anywhere." The man had turned now. Wiry hair frizzed out from beneath the brim of his tall silk hat. His nose was rather long and he had a weak chin. His necktie was scarlet red, which was most unusual among Parisian gentlemen.

"Why is his cravat red?" Sylvie asked.

"I think it's something architects do," Isabel replied. "They are not quite as artistic as, say, painters. So they don't wear berets."

"But Monsieur Degas doesn't wear a beret," Sylvie interrupted.

"He's the exception, I think," Isabel replied. "He wears a tall silk hat like businessmen. Maybe he's a businessman-painter. I don't know. But architects wear them because they have to do business with lawyers and plumbers and stone-masons. So they must look mostly like businessmen. But they want to express a little bit of their artistic side. So they might wear a colorful tie."

"You'd never see a doctor in one of those, would you?" Sylvie mused.

"*Non!* I wouldn't trust a doctor in a red tie," Isabel replied.

Sylvie looked at Isabel and smiled. She certainly had an opinion about everything!

The girls spent a fruitless half hour looking for Giuseppina and then ran to the Comédie-Française. Their hunger always left them as soon as they entered the cavernous space, with its stenches and the gasps of horribly wounded soldiers. Léontine Beaugrand met them practically as soon as they entered and quickly led them to a small room for their food.

"It's not much, girls — a bit of bread, some biscuits. But there is some chocolate and I think a few pieces of dried fruit."

"*Merci*, mademoiselle." Both girls curtsied.

"Now run along. The weather is turning quite cold out there for September. And be careful with those bundles. Don't let anyone know they contain food."

It *was* cold when they left. Sylvie and Isabel said good-bye. They would meet tomorrow and perhaps go to Isabel's apartment to figure out the rest of this dance they would have to make up. *Oh, lies!* Sylvie thought. And now she would have to make up yet another lie to explain to her mother where she had gotten the food.

There was a brisk wind coming off the river as Sylvie walked home. But still the river looked beautiful as twilight gathered. The wind had ruffled its surface into little pleats, gray satin pleats. *How lovely,* Sylvie thought. And this was real water, not painted water, not yard upon yard of the silk sometimes used to imitate a flowing stream. It gleamed now.

She was near the Pont Saint-Michel and walked out onto the bridge to get a better look at the river. She pulled her thin fitted jacket closer around her. She had no shawl. But she wanted to look at the water moving under the bridge. There was something mesmerizing about this water. She forgot about being hungry. She forgot about her lies and she was almost about to forget Giuseppina when she remembered that she had once overheard the ballerina talking to a girl in the *corps* about a shop. A ribbon shop on the Left Bank, near the Pont-Neuf, where she had bought ribbons for toe shoes. Sylvie's eyes flew open as she recalled what the other *corps* dancer had said: "That's very convenient for you!"

If it *was* convenient, it must mean that Giuseppina lived near this shop. Sylvie had never thought of going to the Left Bank; most of the dancers lived on the Right Bank, near the opera house. She must go! She must go right now! Would the ribbon shop still be there? Bakers ran out of flour. Cheese makers ran out of milk. But did ribbon shops run out of ribbons? No one was starving for ribbons in this siege.

Sylvie quickly made her way across the bridge. She turned left and walked down the Rue des Grands Augustins. Just as surely as her instincts led her to stage doors, she now was almost certain that she was in Giuseppina's neighborhood. It was as if there was some invisible compass guiding her, an invisible hand. She instinctively felt that she must again turn left down the Rue Danton. Yes! There was a ribbon shop. The name above the door of the shop read FÉLICE: PURVEYORS OF FINE RIBBONS. The shop was shuttered, so she kept walking, turning left at the corner and making a right through a small alley. It was when she entered the narrow alley that a chill ran up her spine. Stronger than any instinct she had ever experienced, she knew, knew deep within her, that she was being followed.

Now she was truly frightened. The streets in this neighborhood had suddenly become shabby. The buildings looked uninhabited. There was a dead cat in the gutter. Propped against a building was a shamelessly dressed woman, her face thick with rouge. Thick black pencil outlined her eyes, making them appear huge and frightening. Sylvie dashed into another alley. Whoever was following her was close, she knew it. Very close. She crouched behind a dustbin. She curled herself into as tiny a ball as possible, clutching her knees. She felt a shadow pass over her. She clamped her eyes shut tight and willed herself invisible and held her breath. A terrible thought suddenly struck her. *I could be a statue on a grave!*

She heard a scratching sound near her. A rat! She saw its long, thin tail disappear under a small heap of garbage.

"Petit rat! Petit rat!" a voice said softly.

Sylvie's heart seemed to stop. A breath locked in her throat. She began praying silently. *I don't want to be murdered. . . . No, no! This cannot be true,* bon Dieu.

"Petit rat, come out now. *Petit rat! Papa Chat* is here!"

Sylvie's blood ran cold.

Chapter 15

Papa Chat . . . pas de chat . . . Papa Chat? The two tilting green eyes seemed disembodied in the dim light of the alley.

"What are you doing here?" Sylvie whispered hoarsely. The street sweeper was now crouching in front of her. She clutched her bundle of food tightly. He must have been a black marketer. Well, she would give him her food, but luckily, she did not have the lists on her.

"Maybe we have more in common than you think," the sweeper said.

Sylvie could not imagine what that might be. "You've been following me, haven't you?"

"You've been looking for someone — for a long time now, *haven't you?*"

Sylvie was temporarily confused. "I don't have the lists with me. Here, you can have this food." She thrust out the bundle toward him. "Just let me go."

He laughed, dug an old cigarette stub from between the cobblestones, and lit it. His face glowed fiendishly in the light of the match flame.

"Keep your food, little rat. Someone else needs it more."
There was something oddly familiar about the way in which
his voice swooped up at the end of a sentence.

"What are you talking about?"

"You seek the little Italian, *non?*"

"Giuseppina! Yes, Giuseppina Bozzacchi." *That was it!* Sylvie
realized. He sounded like Giuseppina! He must be Italian as
well. That would explain their connection. But a man like this
simply could not be a relative of the beautiful little dancer.

"Follow me, little rat."

"Follow you?"

His laugh now came out as a hiss. "Yes, me, the street
sweeper."

Sylvie followed, walking in the street sweeper's shadow. They
threaded their way through narrow alleys and crossed wall-less
courtyards behind dilapidated buildings.

"We are here," he finally said as they arrived at a building
that swayed on its rotting foundation like a drunkard. "Let me
go first," he said sharply. Sylvie followed him into the building
but instead of going up the stairs, the street sweeper pushed
through a door and began descending into a cellar.

"Wait here!" he told her when they were at the bottom.

It was pitch-black. Sylvie could not see a thing. But she
heard another door creak and saw a crack of light. Then in
another minute the street sweeper was back. She felt a claw
wrap around her wrist. "I will lead you."

"Wait a second," Sylvie said. She tried to swallow her fear. "Are you her father?" she asked tentatively.

The tilting green eyes crinkled up. There was a wild light that seemed to cancel out the gloom. "I only wish I could claim such. No, I am just another Italian."

"Is that how she knew you, then?"

"She likes to speak Italian." The street sweeper gave a harsh cackle. "Yes, even with the likes of me, little rat."

Then, with her heart thumping, Sylvie let herself be pulled through the darkness toward the crack of light.

The door swung open wider. Sylvie's throat constricted. There was a heap of what looked like rags against the wall, but in the middle of the heap was a face as white as a limelight moon. Giuseppina!

"She's dying," a voice croaked from a corner. It was then that Sylvie noticed another figure. She had no idea if the bent, gnarled person wrapped in a black shawl was a man or a woman. Clenched in the person's mouth was a pipe. The glow from its bowl illuminated a lined face with a thin sprouting of hair—not quite a beard—on the chin. A nearly bald head gleamed through a few random strands of hair that had been pulled back into a knot no bigger than a thimble, and absurdly tied with a black velvet ribbon. *From the ribbon shop?* Sylvie wondered. Chantal's taunting words came back to her. "Ah, you are a *sujet*? Or just a *coryphée*? I don't think the girls in the *quadrille* wear such ribbons."

Sylvie moved, as if in a trance, toward where Giuseppina lay. She bent down next to the frail ballerina. Her breathing was ragged, and Sylvie was shocked to see that she was nearly skeletal. Her face was so thin that the outline of her gums and teeth showed through the skin around her mouth.

"Giuseppina!" she whispered softly. She saw something flutter behind the ballerina's eyelids. "Giuseppina, it is me, Sylvie Bertrand. The girl from the opera ballet school. Remember me? I was in *Giselle* . . . just stage furniture . . . I . . . I . . ." Sylvie's voice dwindled. How could she say it? How could she say that she was the girl, the statue on the tombstone of Giselle? It was all becoming dreadfully real. Two worlds were colliding in this damp, cold cellar. She could no longer neatly sort them out. The magic was marrying the real.

The gruesome *pas de deux* had begun: There was a limelight moon provided by a dying girl's face. There was hideous stage furniture — the neither-man-nor-woman sucking on its pipe, and the cat-eyed street sweeper. The last act had already begun, and now, in anticipation of the coda, the music that closed the ballet, the not-man-not-woman had removed the pipe from the mouth hole and leaned forward. So had the street sweeper. Sylvie picked up Giuseppina's hand in her own and pressed it to her lips. She knew that the ballerina was beyond help. The food Sylvie carried would be useless. There was only one thing Sylvie could do, and that was to be there, so that Giuseppina Bozzacchi would not die, abandoned by the ballet world, in this dirty cellar. So she leaned over and began to whisper in her ear.

"I am here, Giuseppina. You are not alone." The ragged breathing began to thunder in Sylvie's ears like a percussion sequence. "We are someplace else. We are in a beautiful forest clearing. You are dancing. I shall make the counts for you." Sylvie had her fingers pressed on Giuseppina's wrist and could feel the pulse growing dimmer. Her pulse made the counts. "*Pas de bourrée . . . bourrée.*" They were floating together. "*Pas de bourrée. . . . now the lovely entrechat. Pas de bourrée . . . bourrée.*" Yes, they were really floating.

Giuseppina's eyes suddenly fluttered open. But the pulse in the wrist Sylvie held beat its last count. Twenty-four counts. Before Sylvie's eyes, Giuseppina Bozzacchi had become Myrtha, the queen of the Wilis. Still holding her hand, Sylvie looked around the cellar. The street sweeper and the figure wrapped in black were gone. So was her bundle. But the spirit of Giuseppina still hovered. Although Sylvie knew that with the first rays of sunlight it would be gone just as Myrtha and her Wilis were forced back into their graves at dawn.

Twenty-four counts. That was what the coda took. Twenty-four counts to die.

Chapter 16

Sylvie was standing between her mother and Léontine Beaugrand on the Place Dauphine. The crisp autumn breezes were said to be perfect for the event about to take place. Sylvie could not quite believe the sight before her. An immense balloon with green and white stripes was tethered by a half dozen ropes. A man was now climbing into the basket suspended beneath the balloon. Sylvie felt Mademoiselle Léontine squeeze her hand. It was Léontine Beaugrand's secret love who was climbing into the basket. His name was Léon Gambetta, and he was the leader of the Third Republic, which was resisting the Prussians.

Sylvia tried to picture the Prussian troops outside the city, encircling it. She imagined it as a noose, and with each day the noose was pulled tighter and tighter around Paris. The city would feel the pressure of strangulation. She heard someone say that less than ninety days of food stores were left for the entire city. Nothing could come in and no one could go out. This was the reason for Léon Gambetta's desperate attempt to escape Paris in a hot-air balloon. It was such a huge gamble Sylvie herself could not imagine taking such a risk. Hopefully, Gambetta would be carried in the balloon into the provinces of France to organize a resistance. Otherwise he might end up God knew where, because of the wind's whimsies.

Sylvie watched as the balloon rose into the flawless blue sky. She tried to imagine what it must be like up there, floating in silence, drifting through the clouds. The Prussians who ringed the city below must look like toy soldiers. The sounds of war would be fading. Gambetta, suspended in his basket, was now between a cloud that looked like a fish swimming in a blue sea and another that resembled an elephant's head. He was close enough to reach out and touch the trunk of the elephant. It was all so strange and fantastical. But no more so than Sylvie's own life had been over the past weeks.

If Sylvie had tried to put together a picture of those weeks, it would have been as jumbled and confusing as the tumbling glass in a kaleidoscope. She kept remembering how she had sat in that miserable cellar holding the hand of the dying Giuseppina. The news of the *danseuse étoile*'s death had swept the ballet world. There were endless questions. Why did no one know that she was starving to death? And was it just starvation? Some said it was cancer. Some said it was pneumonia. But what added an immeasurable dimension of sadness to the tragedy was that the day she had died had, in fact, been Giuseppina's seventeenth birthday. They now called her the Little Doll, for no one would ever forget her debut in *Coppélia*. But for Sylvie, the dancer's most memorable role would always be that of Myrtha, the queen of the ghost spirits in *Giselle*.

Sylvie would also never forget that morning when she had returned to her apartment just after dawn. Her mother had been hysterical with fear, certain that Sylvie had been murdered in the streets of Paris. So there were no more lies after that morning. Sylvie made that vow to herself. She told her mother the entire tale, untangling every false thing she had ever said. She was not sure what stunned her mother more — the fact that she had been helping in the food collection, that she had found Giuseppina dying in the terrible cellar, or that she had lied about herself and Isabel practicing the duet. Her mother had seemed almost dazed as she looked at her. Sylvie knew what she was thinking — *my darling, perfect little girl, my ballerina, my liar!*

Her mother had finally nodded. Not as if she understood. It was just a simple nod. And, from that day on, everything was different. There was, of course, the war and the ongoing siege, but it was more than that. Sylvie's mother was no longer able to deny this real world that her daughter had discovered outside the opera house. She did not disapprove. Sylvie wondered if it had to do with the fact that Mademoiselle Léontine herself was so deeply involved with the war effort. Or maybe her mother was simply afraid that Sylvie would begin to lie again. Perhaps the war itself had come too close to Paris.

Although Léon Gambetta did succeed in escaping, on January 5, Paris began to shake as Prussian guns started to bombard the city.

The day the bombardment began was beautiful, clear, and very cold. Sylvie and her mother were in the courtyard, taking down the laundry that had actually frozen stiff in the bitter temperatures when suddenly, they heard a thunderous series of booms. The cobblestones beneath their feet shook.

"The guns, Mama!" When she had been running her lists, Sylvie had heard talk in the streets of the big caliber Prussian guns. Her mother looked bewildered. "The guns," Sylvie repeated. "The Prussian guns." Yvette began to quickly take down more laundry.

"Mama, leave the laundry! We must get inside."

They raced in the back door of the apartment building and found the other tenants hurrying up and down stairs.

"Stand in a doorway!" a man was yelling. "It's the safest place if they hit the building."

Sylvie and her mother were not sure why, but they raced for the first open doorway they saw. It was that of Madame Tatou, their very fat landlady. They squashed in beside her. Everything seemed to shake. Some grits of plaster rained down from the ceiling. They all looked up. Sylvie looked at Madame Tatou. The creases between her triple chins had melted away, and there was just one fat chin left, trembling to the sound of the booming guns. A mole that had been tucked between the creases was revealed.

That is so ugly. And there are hairs bristling from it! But why am I thinking about Madame Tatou's ugly mole? I might die any second and I am thinking about her mole.

It seemed like hours but it was less than five minutes when the guns finally stopped.

"*Merci*, Madame Tatou," Yvette said softly.

"*De rien*, madame. *De rien.* It is nothing. We must all help each other against these Prussian dogs."

Sylvie wished she had not thought those things about Madame Tatou's mole.

Shakily, Sylvie and her mother made their way upstairs to their apartment.

They both sighed with relief when they walked through the door. Everything seemed to be in order. No plaster had fallen from the ceiling. No broken windows. But one thing was different. The toe shoes that really belonged to Léontine Beaugrand, the ones Sylvie had finally gotten her nerve up to ask her for, had fallen from the nail on the wall onto their bed. Sylvie walked over and picked them up. The nail had fallen out, too. She found it in the folds of the puffy bedcover. She pressed it back into the hole and hung up the toe shoes again, just as they had been before. "Just as before," Sylvie murmured. "Everything just as before."

But whether the Paris Opera Ballet was even standing was a question Sylvie and her mother dared not speak out loud. And what about the new opera house, the Palais Garnier? Would it be destroyed before it was even built? For within the space of days, nearly four hundred people were killed and two hundred buildings were destroyed. Going outside for anything was now unthinkable.

The food supplies had dwindled to a catastrophic level. Sylvie and her mother had not eaten anything for the past four days except for some very hard bread. On a freezing cold morning in January, they sat like shadows at the small round table, staring at the last crust of bread and the moldy rind of cheese. They were both thinking the same thing— whether or not they should eat the pot of marmalade. Yvette Bertrand had tucked the marmalade away earlier in the siege. They now thought of that time when there had been at least a three months' supply of food as nearly heavenly.

But just as they were both having these same thoughts about the marmalade, there was a soft tap on the door.

"Entrez!" Yvette called out.

The door pushed open and Chantal appeared. Sylvie had not seen her sister since that day on the bridge. But she had not forgotten Chantal and her dream. Despite looking as gaunt as Sylvie and her mother did, her eyes were bright and a smile trembled on her lips. *Perhaps her dream has come true*, Sylvie thought. But neither Sylvie nor her mother understood this confounding picture of what could only be described as happy starvation.

"Mama, Sylvie, it's over!"

"What's over?" Yvette asked.

"The siege. It has ended. *Fini*. Some sort of agreement has been made. Food is being brought into Paris as we speak!"

If a ballerina ever did a *grand jeté* from a sitting position, it was Sylvie. She was across the room in one flying leap. "The marmalade!"

"The marmalade!" they all chorused.

Sylvie brought it to the table. Chantal fetched spoons and saucers. Sylvie gave the pot to her mother, but her mother was almost too weak to break the wax seal.

"Here, Mama, I'll do it," said Chantal.

She opened the pot and then pushed it gently toward her mother. Their eyes were fastened on their mother's hand as she pried out the cork plug from the pot. Their stomachs suddenly growled in unison and they all looked at one another and laughed softly. Finally, the plug was out and Yvette dipped a spoon into the marmalade. She put a heaping spoonful on a saucer and began to hand it to Chantal.

"No, you first, Mama." Chantal said softly. Tears glistened in Yvette's eyes. She took the spoonful and ate it, almost daintily. Her eyes closed.

Sylvie and Chantal watched, mesmerized, as gladness spread across their mother's face.

Yvette Bertrand and her two daughters took one hour to eat the twelve-ounce pot of marmalade. It was a meal they would all remember for the rest of their lives.

The siege really *was* over on that January day, but the worst was yet to come.

PART THREE

PARIS 1871
Spring

Chapter 17

"Nonsense!" Yvette Bertrand exclaimed.

Madame Tatou was breathing hard.

"But it is true," she insisted.

"If it's not one problem, it's another. First food and now this!" Yvette exclaimed with disgust.

"Now what, Mama?" Sylvie had just arrived with a basket of laundry from the courtyard. She was wondering whatever could have inspired Madame Tatou to labor up the flights of stairs to their apartment. "Is it the Prussians again?"

"No, my dear," Madame Tatou said, still breathing heavily, her face flushed from the exertion. "Not the Germans, not the Prussians."

"The *communards!*" Sylvie's mother spat out the word. It seemed like her mother was too angry to do anything but fume. Her face was almost as flushed as the landlady's.

"What did they do?" Sylvie asked.

Madame Tatou spoke. "The *communards* are so mad about the peace that they have driven the government of the Third Republic out to Versailles."

"You mean, Monsieur Gambetta?" Sylvie asked.

"All the leaders of the Republic," her mother said.

"But why?" Sylvie asked. "Why are they so mad?" She turned to Madame Tatou.

"They do not like the peace that the Third Republic made with the Germans. They think we gave up too much. They are very angry that the Third Republic allowed Prussians to enter the city last week, and now —"

"Yes, and now!" Yvette blurted out. "Now they have formed this stupidity called the Paris Commune. Overthrown the Third Republic and declared themselves as the government. Well, they're not my government, with all that talk of their so-called fairness and equality! I don't believe it for one minute." Sylvie felt a twinge deep inside her. Surely, this was not the same thing that Chantal had talked about. This sounded much different.

"And they say," Sylvie's mother continued, "that they shall also separate the church from the state and that all church property is now state property. I will never go to church again, not with those filthy *communards* as the landlords!"

Sylvie thought this was a rather toothless threat seeing as her mother hardly ever went to church in the first place.

Over the next few days, there were angry protest marches, strikes, and violence within the city. Yet despite all this, the opera house had not been destroyed or even damaged. It remained standing, if squatly, on the Rue le Peletier. Classes had resumed. Performances were sporadic, but they did occur. In perhaps a resurgence of French patriotism and loyalty, French ballerinas were once again dancing the lead roles that, in previous seasons, had been given to the foreign *danseuses étoiles*.

And now Sylvie once again was in her underwear in the examining room of the *foyer de la danse*. She felt the doctor's fingertips walking up her spine. She tried to look straight ahead and not betray her nervousness. But there were more onlookers this time. In addition to her mother and the ballet mistresses there were two other people: Caroline Venetozza, the new director of the school and the teacher of the most advanced class, and Monsieur Edgar Degas, the artist. The teachers had asked Sylvie's mother's permission for him to attend. Sylvie knew her mother was too nervous to say no. But Monsieur Degas had also turned to Sylvie. "And what about the young Mademoiselle Sylvie?"

"What?" Sylvie had no idea what he was talking about.

"Will it disturb you if I observe this examination? I have never sat in on one. I have painted and sketched so many of these dance examinations without having seen them that I am ashamed of it."

Sylvie had assured the artist that he would not disturb her and was secretly pleased that he would be there. But she was also more nervous.

Now all except Monsieur Degas and Madame Bertrand hovered around Sylvie's spine. The normal six-month intervals between examinations had been stretched to nine due to the war and the siege. Sylvie stood as tall as she could. She had given up on her stretching-by-hanging exercise after a very short time. And she had stopped measuring herself after Giuseppina had died. It had seemed silly to worry about growing tall after she had seen death up close.

But she knew she had grown. She had measured herself that morning.

"Sylvie!" Yvette exclaimed when they stood, dumbfounded, looking at the mark on the door. "It takes nine months to grow a baby and now, miracle of miracles, even a poorly fed child has somehow managed to grow almost two inches during this ridiculous siege. Who would have ever guessed such a thing could happen?"

Now, as the teachers hovered around her, Madame Théodore was saying, "My, my, Sylvie, you have sprouted." Sylvie felt a thrill run through her.

"And her spine is perfectly aligned," the doctor offered.

"Oh, I could have told you that, Doctor," Madame Venetozza said. "From her *barre* exercises, I could see that immediately."

Sylvie's heart was beating so hard now she wondered if everyone in the room could hear it. She tried to flash a smile at her mother.

A minute later, Madame Théodore was absolutely wreathed in smiles as she made her way over to Monsieur Roland, who always played the violin for the examinations.

Sylvie in the meantime had climbed back into her *tutu*. Monsieur Roland nodded and tucked his violin under his chin as Sylvie walked to the center of the room. Then the door creaked open. Léontine Beaugrand hurried in and took a seat next to Madame Venetozza. She smiled quickly at Sylvie, but Sylvie, poised to begin her variation, gave only a fleeting look at her dear *petite mère*.

The music began. Sylvie's arms were down in the position known as the fifth *en bas*. She then rose to *en pointe*, except this time she wore real shoes—no boots. The combination she was about to do was, in fact, based on the first twelve counts of the Dolls' Duet that she had choreographed with Isabel. Only this time it was not a duet but a solo—easier in one sense, for it was just she alone and she did not have to keep her steps synchronized with anyone. But now, of course, there were more combinations and more counts to the combinations. Yes, it had been originally twelve counts to lie, twenty-four to die, but it must be eighty-four to advance, to become a member of the company's lowest rank, a member of the *quadrille*, and no longer simply a student. She had practiced this original solo with Léontine every day for the past two weeks.

Pas de chat! She sprang across the floor. Then *pas de bourrée*. Then a perfectly done *brisé*.

When she had finished, she saw that her mother was holding her face in her hands as if she were about to cry.

✻   ✻   ✻

"A miracle! Sylvie, a miracle!" Yvette Bertrand was sputtering as they made their way down the Rue de la Grange Batelière. "Two inches you grew during the siege and your solo was perfect. *Parfait!* Can you believe it, Sylvie? You are a company member now! You will take performance classes in the *foyer* with the raked floor. Are you ready for that?"

"Yes, Mama. Mademoiselle Léontine has given me private instruction there already."

"Oh, yes, I forgot," Yvette replied. "And you will ascend through the ranks. Quickly, I just know it. The wonder of it all!"

Yes, the wonder of it all! And to think that in a sense it really began with a lie, Sylvie thought.

The crowds were becoming thicker and wilder. "Ah, we must cross here," Yvette Bertrand said. "Those filthy *communards* are up to it again. Why can't they be happy with this peace? We have food in our bellies, art in our theaters. They are complaining about a few lousy francs."

"Shush, Mama, someone will hear you."

Yvette snorted, as if to say, "Who cares?" But Sylvie *did* care. She didn't like any talk of the *communards,* but not for the same reasons as her mother. Every time Sylvie thought of the *communards* and their notions of fairness and equality she remembered her conversation on the bridge with Chantal. And furthermore, it reminded her of the street sweeper. The first time she had ever heard the word *communard* was when she and her mother had been confronted by him that long-ago day in front of the closed opera house.

Sylvie had seen not a trace of the street sweeper since the night that Giuseppina died, but she was sure somehow that he was a *communard*, and probably one of the most violent ones — even if he had befriended Giuseppina. She could never figure out how he had discovered that she, Sylvie, was looking for the Italian ballerina. But it had been obvious that, even if this man was violent, he had in some way cared for Giuseppina. Still, the thought of him unnerved Sylvie. Whenever her mother went on one of her rants against the *communards*, Sylvie, although she knew it was not rational, feared that the sweeper would pop up. Around every corner, she saw his sly cat eyes with their deadly green light, his sneer.

There were rumors now, however, that the French army planned to reconquer Paris — with the help of the Prussians of all people! So the *communards* might be on the run, for they would certainly be the first ones killed if such a thing happened. All over the city were placards that still proclaimed the "obscenity" of the peace the Third Republic had made with the Prussians at Versailles.

Suddenly, as they came to a corner there was a huge, deafening sound. Then the air around them seemed to shatter into a thousand pieces.

"Quick, Mama!" Sylvie yelled, and pulled her mother's arm.

A huge glass window had been shattered by an explosion. Sylvie and her mother were caught in a gale of swirling glass fragments. They ducked their heads and ran, finally pressing themselves against the wall in a narrow alley. Sylvie looked at her mother and gasped. There was a line of blood running down Yvette's face from her forehead. *Mama has been shot! No! Don't die.* "Mama, you are bleeding!" she screamed.

"Nonsense!" her mother shouted. Sylvie blinked at her. "It is nothing but a scratch. I would never let those filthy *communards* kill me! Come, we must get home."

A few days later, Sylvie was not sure if it *was* the *communards* who had, in fact, drawn blood from her mother's forehead. It could have been Republican spies. The news had swept through the city that the French Republican forces had begun an assault on the city.

Chantal arrived one morning with a report.

"The *communards* are dithering," she said over coffee. "If they want to succeed, they should move out now, head for Versailles. The Republican forces are disorganized."

"How do you know all this?" Sylvie asked, her frown dimple flashing. She felt a twinge deep within her, a twinge of fear.

"I have my friends," Chantal said slyly.

Yvette grimaced. "You might have your friends, as you call them, Chantal, but the streets are dangerous. You shouldn't be out and about with all this nonsense going on. There is fighting in every section of the city."

"Yes," Sylvie said. "Don't go out, Chantal, please!"

"That is simply not true, Mama," Chantal said, ignoring

Sylvie's plea. "Here it is safe. And behind the Panthéon, where I live, it is safe. Most of the fighting is around the city hall. Don't worry."

"'Don't worry,' she says!" Yvette muttered. "By the way, your sister has made the corps. She is in the *quadrille*— officially."

"Congratulations—officially!" Chantal laughed. "I hope there is a ballet left to dance in. But I will come back when all this 'nonsense' is over, Mama. *Au revoir.*" She waved almost gaily as she whirled out the door.

Congratulations—officially. Somehow this didn't feel like genuine congratulations to Sylvie. She felt more embarrassed than proud.

Sylvie remembered the marmalade—the taste of it still lingered on her tongue. She could call up the fragile magic of that moment when they had all sat as one loving family, with Chantal as soft and respectful as she had ever been. But now that moment had vanished.

Sylvie once again was perched atop the gravestone on the stage of the opera house watching the Myrtha, the queen of the Wilis, dance. *Who is that dancing?* she wondered. *It looks like Giusepppina.*

"But you're dead, Giuseppina. You can't be dancing!" she cried.

"Hush! Statues can't talk, remember?"

"But dead people can't dance," Sylvie replied. "I am standing on your grave."

"But it is all make-believe, remember? You are standing on a pasteboard gravestone. There is nothing beneath it. I am not buried."

"But you are! You are!"

"I am not!" The voice became harsh as the dancer spun around in a *pirouette*. The blurry face began to change. It was not Giuseppina. It was Chantal!

"Chantal!" Sylvie screeched. "Stop, Chantal!" But Chantal just kept spinning around, laughing raucously.

"Mama's dream! Mama's dream!" she squealed.

"Chantal!"

"Sylvie, wake up! You're having a bad dream." Yvette Bertrand was shaking Sylvie's shoulder. "Wake up, child. Just a bad dream."

Sylvie lifted herself up on one elbow and looked at her mother. "But it was so real, Mama, so real!"

Chapter 18

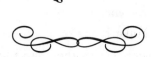

Each day the fighting escalated. The sounds of it came closer and closer. Yvette would not let Sylvie leave the apartment for any reason. It was simply too dangerous. And every time her mother had to go out, Sylvie worried until she heard the footsteps on the stairs.

One morning Yvette, returning from a short errand, brought news that most would have considered disastrous.

"The army of the Third Republic is about to breach the city wall. And you know what, Sylvie?"

"What, Mama?" Sylvie was almost afraid to ask. There was no person more pro-Republican and anti-*communard* than her mother. Not even Léontine Beaugrand, who was the secret love of Léon Gambetta.

"The army from Versailles is more than sixty thousand strong and they say it will soon double because Bismarck, dear man, is giving us more. Yes. He is releasing French prisoners of war! Is that not fantastic?"

Bismarck, dear man? Fantastic?

"Well, Sylvie, what do you think?"

"Mama, I hope you didn't say all that when you were out on your errands. It's dangerous to talk that way, you know. You can't go around calling Bismarck a 'dear man.' In most people's eyes he is the enemy."

"Of course, I know. Don't speak nonsense."

There it was again, her mother's favorite word—*nonsense*.

"No. I'll tell you what is nonsense, Mama," Sylvie said defiantly. "We could all be killed. How do they know the difference between a *communard* and any of us? Tell me that!" Sylvie slapped down the toe shoes on which she had been sewing ribbons. They were her first truly new pair. She had received them the day she had passed the examination.

Yvette regarded her daughter with much the same look she had when Sylvie had told her she was lying. Disbelief. And perhaps there was a dawning awareness that this was not quite the Sylvie she thought she knew.

"Well, it will all be all right. Let's not trouble ourselves about it. All this will be done in a few days," Yvette said quietly as she unpinned her hat.

Yvette was right. It was all "done" in a few days. Between May 21 and May 28, the Versailles troops of the Republicans had slaughtered unarmed citizens and *communards*. But the worst was what Sylvie heard in the foyer of their apartment building as she returned from the courtyard with a basket of dry laundry.

"They what?" Madame Tatou slapped a hand over her mouth in shock. She was speaking to the tenant who had shouted at them all to run for a doorway when the Prussians had fired the big guns four months before.

"Yes, *c'est fini!*" The man made a cutting gesture across his throat. "At Ménilmontant, against the wall of the Père-Lachaise Cemetery."

"What against the wall of the cemetery?" Sylvie blurted out, her arms locked around the laundry basket.

Madame Tatou and the tenant exchanged glances. "It's not for young ears," whispered Madame Tatou. The tenant shrugged.

Sylvie set down her basket. "No, you must tell me. I am not too young. I want to know." Her dark eyes seemed to grow darker while the gold flecks glinted with a strange ferocity. She felt a coldness seep through her.

The tenant took a step toward her. He had sad, drooping eyes. Everything about him seemed to droop.

"My dear," he began in a low, somewhat creaky voice. "Do you know what a *communard* is?"

"I think, a little." Sylvie bit her lip slightly. "It's a person who is a member of the Paris Commune."

"Yes, and they are very angry because of the peace Monsieur Thiers and Monsieur Gambetta and all the other messieurs of the Third Republic agreed to with the Prussians. They feel that we have been sold out. I don't know. Perhaps they are right." He shrugged again. "I do know that in spite of their high ideals, their courage, and their passion, they are revolutionaries, anarchists. Today they were put an end to."

"Put an end to?" Sylvie leaned toward the man and looked up into his eyes. "You mean killed?"

He nodded. "I mean massacred. At Père-Lachaise Cemetery."

Sylvie raised her hand and pressed it to her mouth. "But that is terrible." She felt her own hot breath against her fingers. "Just because they were anarchists?" Sylvie realized that she might know what the word *communard* was but she did not know the word *anarchist*. "Is an anarchist a murderer?"

"No more so than the Prussians or the army of the Third Republic who slaughtered them."

"But why were they murdered?"

"For their beliefs, my dear, for their beliefs."

Sylvie bent over and picked up the laundry basket. *For beliefs, people are murdered. For beliefs. This is indeed unbelievable!*

Chapter 19

I'll be back when this nonsense is over. Like a dim echo, Chantal's words seeped through Sylvie's mind. This moment simply could not be happening. There was a tawdry woman standing in their apartment, her cheeks rouged a vile color of pink. Her eyes were outlined thickly and her bright red lips sat on her face like a squashed rose. From that battered flower came words that simply made no sense at all.

"Chantal was just in the wrong place at the wrong time. She was killed in a sudden crossfire. Instantly. No pain."

Was there a fleeting shadow behind the scrim of the painted eyes? Sylvie was not sure. She felt her mother sway. Their shoulders touched.

"Sit down, Mama. Sit down."

"Are you sure?" Yvette Bertrand asked.

The woman nodded, "Yes, madame."

"Where is she?"

"You mean—" The woman hesitated. "Her body?"

"Yes, her body," Yvette said with a sob.

Body. Chantal is a body. This isn't right. Chantal cannot be just a body.

"Well, madame . . . it . . . it"—the woman hesitated again—"it simply disappeared," she answered quickly. *Too quickly*, Sylvie thought. "But I have something for Sylvie."

"For me?" Sylvie asked.

"Yes, Chantal said that if anything ever happened to her, you were to have these." From her purse she pulled a small package. "Here." She thrust out the brown paper package.

Sylvie untied the string and folded back the paper. Two frayed pink ribbons and the black velvet throat ribbon Chantal had worn as a member of the *coryphée* lay in the crinkles of the paper.

"Why?" Sylvie whispered.

"She wanted you to have them," the woman repeated.

Chantal wanted me to have them . . . in case anything happened? What did she think was going to happen? Sylvie wondered. The ribbons blurred through her tears.

"Ah, Sylvie," her mother said, and touched the ribbons.

"I must go," the other woman said. Then she turned and left.

Sylvie continued to look at the ribbons for perhaps another minute. *If anything ever happened to her.* Had her mother simply been too stunned to find those words odd?

"Mama," she said suddenly. "I'll be right back."

"Where are you going? Don't leave me, Sylvie."

"Don't worry, Mama, I'll be right back," she repeated as she threw on a knit shawl and raced out the door.

If she hurried she could catch up with the woman, but she couldn't tell her mother this. If she missed the woman, she could go to the street Chantal lived on, behind the Panthéon, and find her. The woman would cross the river most likely at the Pont Marie. Sylvie could stop her on the bridge.

Sylvie spotted the figure ahead. *But what is she doing? That's not the way to the bridge.* She began running toward her. "Mademoiselle! Mademoiselle!" She didn't even know her name! "Mademoiselle," she called a third time as she ran up behind her and tapped her shoulder. The woman stopped. Sylvie was almost out of breath. Gasping, she said, "I have to ask you a question."

"Yes?" the woman replied, looking at her suspiciously.

"You said Chantal wanted me to have the ribbons in case something happened to her. What do you mean? Why did she think something might happen to her?"

The woman suddenly looked very uncomfortable. Casting her eyes down toward the sidewalk, she replied, "She made me promise not to tell."

It was then that Sylvie realized the truth about Chantal. "She was a *communard*, wasn't she?"

The woman nodded. "She said it would kill your mother to know."

"But it killed Chantal, didn't it?" Sylvie replied. *And,* thought

Sylvie, *Chantal said that she would die for the right cause.* Tears were now streaming down her face. "Père-Lachaise?" she asked.

The woman nodded again. "She was killed at Père-Lachaise. That is why there is no body. God knows what they did with them."

"I see," Sylvie said.

"Here," the woman held out a handkerchief to her.

Sylvie took it and dabbed her eyes. "Don't worry, I won't tell my mother." She paused. "One thing, though." The question, she realized, might seem silly, but she had to know.

"Yes?"

"How come you didn't take the bridge? Don't you live near where Chantal lived? Behind the Panthéon?"

"Oh, no. We lived together in Les Halles."

"What? Les Halles?" *The meat market!* Sylvie could hardly believe it. Butchers and all sorts of low-life people lived there.

The woman shrugged and gave an odd little smile. "She said your mother wouldn't like that, either."

"No, not at all." Sylvie's voice was leaden.

The woman began to walk away. Sylvie watched her. She turned at the next corner. That, of course, would be the most direct route to Les Halles.

PART FOUR

PARIS 1873
Autumn

Chapter 20

Sylvie had just finished a string of *pas de bourrées* across the stage floor. She stood now in the second row of the *corps* while Camille Fontaine danced the role of Myrtha, Queen of the Wilis.

Sylvie's filmy peach silk tunic, sprinkled with pearls, stirred around her from the pumped wind that blew the fog. From her shoulders, almost like wings, a cape of translucent tulle floated. The storm of butterflies that had raged in Sylvie's stomach as she waited in the wings had now been tamed. She had, for that brief moment, envied the lighting man, the stagehands, the dressers who made sure their headpieces stayed on and their *tutus* were just right. All these people could stay behind the curtain unseen. If they made a mistake no one saw *them* — just the mistake. But if *she* made a mistake, like a bad landing from a jump, so bad that she went splat on the stage, everyone would see it. But in the next second she was scolding herself. *I am a Wili! You have always wanted this, Sylvie. How can you envy a stagehand? You will not go splat!*

No, she would not go splat but something very peculiar

was happening now. Sylvie stood with her arms delicately crossed on her chest and her head bent down, in the melancholy pose of a Wili. She blinked as she saw a glistening, small stream of liquid begin to make its way down the raked stage toward the orchestra pit. Mon Dieu, *this cannot be happening!* Ghislaine, an older girl in the corps, had said just as they lined up in the wings that she had to pee. Sylvie heard a snicker to one side of her. This *was* happening! Ghislaine was peeing onstage. There was another snicker and then not a storm of butterflies but an absolute blizzard of giggles began to rise in Sylvie. *I must not laugh! I must concentrate. I must look melancholy. I have to begin another set of* pas de bourrée *and then a* glissade. *A glissade on pee? I'll slip!* She pressed her lips together more firmly. She began biting her tongue. The *pas de bourrée* would start on the third count of eight. Isabel was right behind her.

She could hear Isabel breathing but not laughing. Both she and Isabel had been onstage many times by now, but never in such a select group of the *coryphées* as the Wilis. And to think someone had actually urinated onstage! Well, so far the audience hadn't noticed. They must carry on. Of all the scary stage stories Sylvie had heard, about falling dancers—and even when Rita Sangalli had miscalculated the depth of a stage in a foreign country and did a *grand jeté* right into the orchestra pit—she had never heard one about someone peeing onstage. *Flûte!* She must stop thinking about this. This was not the worst thing that could happen on a stage. She had seen that worst thing—at the Comédie-Française, a stage streaked with the blood of dying men. Sylvie swallowed as she began the *glissade*, and her laughter died within her.

(When Sylvie left the stage that evening, it was not her toes that were bleeding, it was her tongue. She had bitten it so hard that her teeth had actually drawn blood.)

There was, however, to be no more dying in the Comédie-Française. Peace had finally been restored to Paris, to France. France was smaller with the losses of Alsace and Lorraine, which had been formally ceded to Germany in the treaty. And people were still bitter about that. People spoke of *revanche*, or revenge. In fact, there was a movement called *revanchism*, aimed at punishing past enemies and regaining former territory. But so far no one had taken revenge. Eight months before, in February, France had officially become a republic.

Certain memories of those horrible days under the siege had dimmed for Sylvie. Some had not. She would never forget the death of Chantal and the secret knowledge Sylvie possessed and must *never* reveal to her mother. Nor would she ever forget Giuseppina. It was not as hard as she had thought it would be watching Camille Fontaine dance the role of Myrtha. Not at all, really. Camille looked like a cow attempting a Scottish jig next to Giuseppina. She did not float. She more or less plopped. Sylvie was relieved. The memory of Giuseppina as Myrtha remained untarnished. Sylvie had lived *Giselle* all too literally, and Giuseppina had found both her own mortality and immortality within it.

The second set of eight counts was approaching. One, two,

three . . . Sylvie stepped into the limelight in front of eight hundred people. She felt her cape of translucent tulle begin to float away from her shoulders. *I must float. I must float.* She began her *pas de bourrée* across the stage. She remembered Mademoiselle Léontine's words from rehearsal. *It is like petit point, Sylvie, like petit point. Tiny, tiny stitches. You are embroidering magic out there. . . .*

Yes, magic, Sylvie thought as she floated across the stage. *I am embroidering magic!*

Sylvie Bertrand, member of the *coryphée* of the Paris Opera Ballet, was back in that world of magic. There was the dry, pungent scent of the carpentry shop. She had missed that, and the strange geometry of the flats, painted to look three-dimensional so that villages appeared to have depth and trees circumferences.

This autumn had been exciting. She had had many private instructions with Mademoiselle Léontine. In fact, during one of these classes, the great architect Charles Garnier had walked in. Sylvie had been going into a fourth rotation of a *pirouette* when she saw a blur of red in the corner. It was Monsieur Garnier with his red necktie. She later learned that the architect had not come to measure the room; he was a good friend of Léontine Beaugrand's and he had brought her a present, which Mademoiselle Léontine showed Sylvie after her class.

It was a book, *Gulliver's Travels* by Jonathan Swift. When Sylvie opened the book, she saw an amazing engraving. It showed a huge man tied to the earth with ropes and hundreds of tiny little people around him.

"What is this?" Sylvie asked.

"Those are the Lilliputians and that is Gulliver."

"But what is this story about?"

"Ah, you must read it to find out. I'll tell you a little. Gulliver is a voyager, a traveler, and he encounters this race of little people called Lilliputians. You see, here in this picture, he is just waking up after being shipwrecked. And these little people have tied him down with hundreds of tiny threads."

"The little people are his captors, then?" Sylvie asked. Mademoiselle Léontine nodded. "Is it a funny book?"

"It is what is called satire. It makes fun of things."

"What kinds of things?"

"Mighty people, nations, armies, power."

Sylvie paused. Was what had happened, this war with the Prussians, a satire? After the blood she had seen smeared across the stage of the Comédie-Française, she couldn't understand how anyone could make fun of war.

"Do the Lilliputians kill Gulliver?" Sylvie asked.

"Oh, no. They find him fascinating."

"Do they ever untie him?"

"Yes. And they take him to meet their emperor. And soon they begin to use him as a kind of national resource."

"What do you mean — national resource?"

"Well, they use his bigness in their wars against another

small race. But then he gets in trouble and that is very funny indeed."

"What happens, what happens? Tell me!"

"I'll tell you if you promise to read the book someday."

Sylvie suddenly remembered Chantal telling her how she had learned to read books. "I will, I will. My reading has improved so much. Please tell me the funny thing."

"Well, he is arrested."

"What for?"

"For treason." Léontine Beaugrand put her hand to her mouth and began to giggle. "For putting out a fire in the royal palace with his urine."

"Non!" They both started laughing raucously. "What happens to him?"

"He is condemned to be shot in the eyes with poisoned arrows."

"Oh, no! Do they?"

"I won't tell you. You'll have to read the book."

"Can I take it home with me today?"

"Today? I thought Monsieur Mérante needed to see you this evening."

"Oh, I forgot!" Sylvie wondered how she could have ever forgotten such an important meeting with the most distinguished teacher of the performance classes.

Louis Mérante had choreographed a new ballet, *Gretna Green*, based on a Scottish folktale. It was a very romantic story about two lovers who run away so that they can marry.

The ballet was not the most beautiful nor the most exciting, but it was fun being part of the process of choreography. Sylvie's role was not large, but Monsieur Mérante spent a long time trying out combinations on the dancers. And Sylvie, although just in the corps, was one of his favorite corps members for trying out a combination. It was not unlike having a fitting with Madame Preschinka, the costume designer, who would say, "Turn this way, dear. Is that comfortable or too tight? Can you move?" Whereas Monsieur Mérante would say, "Try the *pas de bourrée* for, say, eight counts and then the *glissade*. Does that feel better, more natural?"

Instead of fitting a costume to the body, Monsieur Mérante was fitting dance to the body. The costume designer and the choreographer simply used different fabrics — one cloth, the other movement. And neither Madame Preschinka nor Monsieur Mérante would insist that a combination or a feature of a costume be followed simply because they had thought it up. If it didn't work for the dancer, then it didn't work at all. For that, in fact, was their work — to make things work seamlessly, effortlessly. That was the true aesthetic of ballet.

Sylvie had learned all this in the past two years. And it was, of course, the essence of magic. No one realized that the trees were flat, that the street that wound through the village went nowhere. No one saw the brushstrokes, or the stitches, or the seams. They only saw the steps. So the steps must be wonderful.

Chapter 21

For all the magic that Sylvie had returned to in the opera house, she had not forgotten the real world outside. She still made forays into this world. She still loved the fragility of real leaves and the way the light could shine through their pale green in earliest spring. She loved the Seine, which flowed like liquid satin through Paris, and the tightly furled roses in the summer gardens of the Tuilleries.

Sylvie now walked by herself all the time to and from the opera house, without her mother. Sylvie's mother had taken a permanent position with the comtesse Mercier at her house on the Rue du Faubourg Saint-Michel. On her way home Sylvie often stopped on the bridge at exactly the same spot where she and Chantal had met that day, when Chantal had told her about beginning to have a new dream, a dream of fairness and equality. A dream that had killed her. Sylvie often wondered about Chantal's friend Catherine, who taught her to read. What might she have been like?

This morning, as Sylvie walked toward the opera house

along the Rue de Richelieu, a maverick leaf of astonishing color blew into her path. She stooped to pick it up. How lovely. This was precisely what was needed for one of the scenes in *Gretna Green*. Madame Preschinka had been complaining about "too much plaid . . . plaid is basically ugly!" The ballet premiered in three weeks. Madame Preschinka had been working day and night to prepare the costumes, and she had said that she was stuck on what the six members of the corps should wear in the second act. *This leaf might help her,* Sylvie thought.

"Hello!" Isabel ran up to Sylvie as she turned into the Rue de la Grange Batelière. "What have you got there?" she asked.

"A leaf. You know, a real leaf?" They both laughed when Sylvie said this.

"But why?" Isabel asked.

"Does there have to be a reason to pick up a pretty leaf?"

"No. I suppose not."

"But there is."

"Sylvie," Isabel said with mock exasperation. "You are talking in riddles this morning. So what *is* the reason?"

"It is not plaid."

"*Flûte!*" Isabel exclaimed. "That really is a riddle."

"Come on, I'll explain later."

Five minutes later, Sylvie and the four other girls in the wedding dance of the second act were chattering away, waiting for Madame Preschinka. For Sylvie the costume *atelier* in many ways was the heart of this world that manufactured fantasy. There were trunks and boxes overflowing with fabrics. *Tutus* in various stages of construction hung from clotheslines like air spirits. Then there were cubbyholes with trimmings — lavish beading, false jewels — and there was one small room just for feathers. Madame Preschinka soon bustled into the room with Monsieur Mérante. She was a large, corpulent woman and her corsets did little to reduce her girth.

"But, Monsieur Mérante," she was complaining. "As I told you before, there is simply too much plaid in this second act. I am making the plaid as romantic as possible by using the chiffon, but still there is something else needed to weave through the plaid."

"Madame?" Sylvie interrupted.

"What is it, Sylvie?"

Sylvie held up the leaf. It was a deep russet with a patch of gold on one edge.

Madame Preschinka's eyes almost popped from her head. "*C'est ça!* That's it! I shall make them look like autumn leaves blowing through the wind. Yes, quick. My sketchbook." She snapped her fingers and an assistant came running with her book and a handful of colored pencils. Within a few minutes, she had sketched tunics that were to be composed of "leaves" of chiffon in hues of russet, gold, and olive.

"Ah!" Monsieur Mérante said, looking over her shoulder. "I like it. You were right about too much plaid."

"Yes, plaid is for schoolgirls, plaid is everyday — at least in Scotland. But people come to the ballet to see romance, not schoolgirls."

It was the opening night of *Gretna Green*. Sylvie, Isabel, and the other four "leaves," as they were now being called, had just finished their dance to great applause. But when they exited into the wings, they saw Madame Preschinka scowling and Monsieur Mérante scratching his chin. *Had they done that poorly?* Sylvie wondered. The people had applauded vigorously when they had finished. "What did we do wrong?" Genevieve, a russet leaf, asked.

"Not you, my dear. *Moi!*" Madame Preschinka cried. "More layers, Monsieur Mérante, many more layers. The lime-lights take density from the hues, as well as the delicacy. The hues appear flat, too cool, not warm. *Frou-frous!* That is the answer," she said, raising a finger into the air as an exclamation point.

"But can you redo them by tomorrow night's performance?" Monsieur Mérante asked.

"If the girls will stay late after tonight's performance, I can do it."

"Yes, yes, madame," they all chorused.

At midnight, six very tired "leaves" were standing in the costume *atelier* while Madame Preschinka, with a mouthful of pins, was fitting them with hastily basted together *frou-frous*, the layers of swirling petticoats that added buoyancy to any costume.

These were not the *frou-frous* made famous by the high-kicking cancan girls of Le Moulin Rouge. These were made of the softest chiffon and not stiff faille; they would swirl and move with the dancer. That Madame Preschinka could construct such a *frou-frou* would be a *tour de force*, but Sylvie knew she was determined to do so. And rarely was Madame Preschinka thwarted in her determination.

It was the "leaf" Geneviève who first smelled the smoke. "Is someone smoking in here?"

"*Non*." Madame Preschinka scowled. It was strictly forbidden to smoke in the costume *atelier*. It was much too dangerous with all the fabrics.

"But . . ." She wrinkled her nose. A horrified look crossed Madame Preschinka's face. And at that very moment thick smoke, nearly black, poured through the door. Sylvie's eyes began to sting. There was a sudden, terrible smell. "Feathers! Feathers burning!" Madame screeched.

"Fire!" Someone screamed.

There would be no *frou-frous*. There would be no other performances of the Scottish folktale that Louis Mérante had brought to life. *Gretna Green* on the evening of October 27 was the last ballet ever performed at the Paris Opera on the Rue le Peletier.

The girls, Madame Preschinka, and her assistants ran coughing from the *atelier*, blinded by smoke and gasping for air. The opera house was burning!

Chapter 22

"Sylvie! Sylvie, where are you?"

"Here! Here, Madame Preschinka." Sylvie began to cough. The smoke was so thick one could hardly see. She heard the screams of other people. Even at midnight, the opera house was never really empty. Carpenters, stagehands, scenery painters were there long into the night and often through the dawn during the season.

People were running everywhere, seeking tunnels through the smoke to an exit. Windows were being shattered. Sylvie held Madame Preschinka's hand tightly. The old woman moved slowly. She was gasping. "Sylvie, you run on, my dear. I am too old."

"No! No, madame. I can't leave you here."

Madame Preschinka sighed. She could get no more words out. Neither would Sylvie waste any precious breath on words. A smear of orange appeared overhead. Flames leaped in the night on the other side of a high window. Sylvie suddenly knew where they were: not far from the stage door. Even through the thick smoke, Sylvie still possessed her instinct for stage doors.

"This way!" she cried hoarsely. Something bumped into her, soft as a leaf. It *was* a leaf! And then another and another. It was Isabel and Geneviève and Simone, Éloise, and Marie-France. The leaves. They were all here together!

"I know the way to the stage door from here," Sylvie cried. "Follow me." But at just that moment, she was pulled down to the floor. Madame Preschinka had collapsed. Whether she had fainted or was dead, Sylvie did not know.

"We must move her!" she shouted.

"How can we?" Marie-France said. "Look at how big she is. She must weigh at least two hundred pounds!"

But Sylvie suddenly thought of the book that Mademoiselle Léontine had shown her, *Gulliver's Travels*. The Lilliputians! The leaves were like the Lilliputians. They could move Madame Preschinka!

"Yes, we can. We must all try together. Geneviève, Marie-France, you go to that side. Simone, take her head. I'll take her feet. Isabel and Éloise, on this side. All right, on the count of three, we lift."

"One . . . two . . . three . . . *levez!*"

The massive woman rose a foot from the floor, and the girls staggered forward, with Sylvie leading the way. The roar of the fire was deafening. Suddenly, there was a mighty crash as part of the roof fell in. Then a huge wind. For a second, they seemed sucked into a vortex of hot air. Each leaf forgot about the pain in her arms and in her back. Their eyes were streaming, but Sylvie kept yelling, "Not far! Not far!"

Just as the last part of the roof fell in, they came through the stage door. The fire brigade looked shocked when they saw the leaves. They immediately ran to help and picked up Madame Preschinka. Putting her on a stretcher, they ran with her to a carriage ambulance. The leaves ran after them, as far from the tremendous heat of the fire as they could get. There were hundreds of people crowding the Boulevard Haussmann, watching the spectacular blaze. Policemen were holding the crowds back to make way for the firefighters.

"Look, there is Monsieur Mérante!" Sylvie tried to shout, but her voice was scratchy from the smoke. She looked back at the opera house. The sky glowed red around the flaming skeleton of the building. Even the stars seemed to flinch. It was unbelievable to Sylvie that this world that had been her life, which contained all that her mother had dreamed of, was now being destroyed, was dying before her very eyes. At that moment, Louis Mérante came running up to them.

"My leaves! My darling leaves! Are you all right? Are you safe?"

"Yes," they all answered.

"And Madame Preschinka?"

"We hope she is all right. They took her in an ambulance," Geneviève replied.

"Grâce à Dieu!" the choreographer murmured. *"Grâce à Dieu!"*

There was one final, huge explosion and the east and north walls — the very walls that had held the *foyer de la danse* — fell.

The opera house burned for another day. But it smoldered for weeks and, as someone observed, the squat building that had housed an industry of fantasy looked now like a charred plaster cage.

THE CODA

PARIS
June 14, 1876

Sylvie stood in the wings of the new Palais Garnier theater. Its completion had been accelerated because of the fire that destroyed the old opera house. Sylvie was about to dance the role of Sylvia for Louis Mérante's newest ballet in the overwhelmingly beautiful Palais Garnier. The theater had opened in January, but this ballet was being performed in June. The lighting of the lush forest onstage was beautiful, with a soft lavender suggestion of dusk. The flats of trees, with their pale green silk leaves, trembled. A half-dozen nymphs in chiffon pastel tunics with net caps came to life slowly as they began a swirling dance through the trees. The pace quickened. They became more animated, dancing almost flirtatiously.

Sylvie felt someone behind her arranging the flowers in her hair. She turned and smiled at Madame Preschinka. She loved this costume. The flowers that began at the neckline swept in a garland to her waist. The petals made from silk were as delicate as those of real flowers and would flutter in the breeze of her dancing.

This was Sylvie Bertrand's hardest role yet. As Sylvia, she must be the huntress and very powerful, yet at the same time vulnerable. She must dance aggressively, yet delicately. She must show abandon, yet reserve. And this was to be her awakening.

Sylvie was simply shocked when Louis Mérante had come up to her that day, a year before, in the temporary quarters of the Paris Opera Ballet and asked to speak with her.

"I want you for the lead in my new ballet," he had said.

"What is it called?" Sylvie had asked.

"Sylvia."

"You didn't choose me just for the name, did you, *monsieur le maître?*"

"Not just." He smiled softly. Sylvie had wondered what he meant by that. "I must admit that, of course, when I did decide to name the ballet *Sylvia* you did come to mind. That would be foolish to deny. But, my dear, you are right for the role. You have the balance." Sylvie knew that he did not simply mean the ordinary kind of balance that allows a dancer to pose for seemingly endless moments in a gravity-defying equilibrium. No, it was a different kind of balance altogether.

And he explained the story of a huntress, and a shepherd who is obsessed with her, but whom she shoots with her arrow. When he had finished the story, Sylvie touched the velvet ribbon around her neck.

"C'est triste," she murmured.

"Yes, it's very sad, but hopeful, my dear. Awakening a spirit is always hopeful."

"Does this mean that I am promoted to a *première danseuse?*"

"*Non,* my dear."

"*Non?*" A look of fear flooded Sylvie's dark eyes.

"You will be *une danseuse étoile!*"

"*Une danseuse étoile!*"

Once more now, in the wings of the stage, Sylvie touched the ribbon her sister had left for her. Madame Preschinka said she could wear it if she wanted to. She closed her eyes and took a few slow breaths. There was so much more, she realized, than just the steps. There was so much that she had to express. There was so much that made the difference between a dancer in the *corps* and *une danseuse étoile.* She must dance not simply with her feet but with her soul, and that spirit must flow from her like the ribbon she wore. She touched it lightly once again as she peered out at the audience. She saw the man with the short beard in the third row. Monsieur Degas. Was he going to paint her? Sylvie wondered. *Will he paint my soul? Will he capture my spirit?*

She began the counts. There would be just twenty-four more until she made her entrance. Eight counts now. Sylvie arranged her feet once again, left foot forward, with the toe just touching the stage. She was ready to step out. The second to the last count. One thought filled her head now — *This is not Mama's dream. This is mine!*

Sylvie gathered her strength, then burst from the wings in a magnificent *grand jeté.* The audience gasped as a new star glimmered in the lavender twilight of the Palais Garnier.

Author's Note

Dancing Through Fire is a work of fiction, but it is rooted in history. As a writer of historical fiction, I have worked within a framework where facts are used and, on occasion, transcended. I would like to be as clear as possible as to what facts I have based my story on and what facts I have altered. When I have changed facts, I have always tried to remain faithful to the historical period in which they occurred. They have not been changed to undermine history but, rather, to serve the purposes of storytelling. It would not be good storytelling if the essential fabric of the historical period was sacrificed in the process.

Some characters in this story have been made up, while others really did live during these times. Edgar Degas was a real painter in the nineteenth century. He became perhaps most famous for his paintings, drawings, and pastels of dancers of the Paris Opera Ballet. He spent a great deal of time in the *foyer de la danse*, where classes and rehearsals were conducted, in the audience of the theater, and later in the wings of the stage.

He began painting ballerinas in the early 1870s. This coincided with the outbreak of the Franco-Prussian War. Sometimes the dancers who were the subjects of his paintings were identified; other times they were not. The dancer in the painting *L'Étoile*, to the best of my knowledge, has never been identified. I called her Sylvie Bertrand. She is an entirely made-up character but she is modeled on what I learned through extensive research on the lives of the *petits rats*. Her sister, Chantal, as well as her mother are also made up.

Many of the other dancers mentioned, such as Léontine Beaugrand, are real. Léontine did, in fact, become deeply involved in the hospital at the Comédie-Française. Giuseppina Bozzacchi was real as well and was the first ballerina to dance the role of Swanilda in *Coppélia*, which debuted that spring of 1870. Tragically, she died of apparent starvation during the first days of the siege. Many of the teachers at the school, such as Louis Mérante, Jules Perrot, and Caroline Venetozza are also real. Marie du Bac is not a real character but based on Marie van Goethem, who posed for one of Degas's most famous works, the statue *Little Dancer*.

The performance repertory of the ballets is accurate. *Coppélia* was premiered in May 1870. The last ballet to be performed in the opera house on the Rue le Peletier was *Gretna Green*, and the first ballet to be performed in the Palais Garnier was indeed *Sylvia*, but the lead role was danced by an Italian ballerina, Rita Sangalli.

The chronology of the Franco-Prussian War and the Siege of Paris are accurate. Léon Gambetta was one of the leaders of the Third Republic. The relationship between Gambetta and Léontine Beaugrand is a product of my imagination, but Gambetta's fantastic escape from Paris in a balloon is not. He really did leave Paris in a hot-air balloon to rally supporters in the provinces for an army.

After the peace, there were many in Paris who felt that France had sold out. They were particularly upset by the ceding of the provinces of Alsace and Lorraine to Germany. These people formed the Paris Commune and were opposed to the Third Republic founded by Gambetta and Adolphe Thiers, who was its leader.

The Third Republic was afraid that the members of the Paris Commune would arm themselves from the arsenals of the French National Guard. In the artillery of Montmartre, there was a two-hundred-gun battery. On March 18, French troops of the Republic entered Paris, with, it was said, the tacit approval of the Prussians, to seize all the arms within the city. But the National Guard refused to give up their arms, and the leaders of the Republic, including Léon Gambetta, were forced to flee to Versailles. A few days later, a new municipal council was formed, and on March 28, the Paris Commune was proclaimed the new government. They quickly moved to end conscription into the standing army and put a delay on all rents.

Shockingly, with the help of the Prussians, it was now the

Third Republic that declared war on their own city, to wrest it from the *communards.* The final defeat of the Paris Commune came at Ménilmontant, on the east side of the city, where the last of the *communards* were rounded up and shot against a wall in Père-Lachaise Cemetery.

Thirty thousand people in all were massacred within seven days. The numbers of the dead exceeded all of those killed during the Reign of Terror of the French Revolution. The Reign of Terror, however, lasted just short of a year, whereas this new terror lasted a mere week. A week that came to be called *la semaine sanglante* or *bloody week.*

Amazingly, throughout all of these political upheavals the Paris Opera Ballet closed only a few times. I was intrigued by the juxtaposition of art and violence, the realities of war and the fantasy of the stage, the horror and the beauty that coexisted in a delicate balance for almost a year and a half.

I tried to represent as accurately as possible this world of the Paris Opera Ballet. There were four ranks in the company through which a ballerina ascended before becoming a star, if she became a star at all. Students could sometimes be called up for what I have termed "stage furniture" roles and would be paid ten *sous* for a performance.

There are some small but important differences to note between the contemporary ballet world and that of the nineteenth century. First of all, the *tutus* that I refer to were much longer than the ones we think of now. We now call *tutus* of this length "romantic" *tutus,* and they come to midcalf, or just above the knees, as Degas has shown them. Leotards as we now know them did not exist. Students took class in these "romantic" *tutus* and there were rules about how long the tails of a sash could be.

Although the class dress and costumes were somewhat different from what we know today, many of the nonsynthetic fabrics were the same and the construction of these beautiful confections of tulle and silk and chiffon was fairly consistent. I learned most of what I have written about the costumes from the book *Karinska* by Toni Bentley. Madame Barbara Karinska was a legendary costume designer who worked with the renowned choreographer George Balanchine creating costumes for the New York City Ballet.

In Edgar Degas's first painting of dancers, the ballerinas were in the background, and mostly their legs were visible. In the foreground was the orchestra, and from that perspective, we must assume that Degas himself was sitting right behind the orchestra pit. This was 1870. In that same year, he began observing some of the classes, but much of what Degas painted and sketched came from the images he carried away in his imagination from both the *foyer de la danse,* or the rehearsal rooms, and the stage. In fact, he seemed to be singularly devoted to the old Paris Opera House on the Rue le Peletier, and even after it burned he incorporated architectural details of its *foyer de la danse* in his paintings.

It was not until the 1880s that Degas gained the privilege of going backstage and observing from the *coulisses*, the wings. And the words he spoke during the scene of Sylvie's examination are said to be his actual words when he confessed to a friend his regret and embarrassment over never having observed an examination up to that point in his career.

Degas's paintings of the ballerinas were an immediate success and he painted more and more of them over the years. Degas was apparently mesmerized by the intersection between the fantastical world of the ballet and that of the real world. He was fascinated by the transformation of the ballerinas from creatures sweating and "puffing like steam engines" in class to magical, fairylike creatures in a performance.

From hours of watching the ballerinas exercise at the *barre* he became attuned to the nuances and refinements of movement. A French journalist of the time gave this account of seeing Degas at work:

"The rehearsal was in full sway: *entrechats* and *pirouettes* followed one after the other with vigorous regularity in a laborious tension. . . . Degas comes here in the morning. He watches all the exercises in which movements are analyzed, he establishes by successive features the various gradations, half tempos, and all the subtleties. When evening comes, at the performances, when he observes an attitude or a gesture, his memories of the morning recur and guide him in his notations, and nothing in the most complicated steps escapes him. . . . He has an amazing visual memory." (François Thiebault-Sisson)

It was Degas's unique memory of movement that allowed him to observe the performance of a ballerina such as Sylvie and carry every step in his imagination back to the canvas in his studio.

The Degas painting that inspired this novel is called *L'Étoile*, or, *The Star* (and is also known as *Dancer on the Stage*). Completed in 1878, this beautiful painting now hangs in the Musée D'Orsay in Paris.

Acknowledgment

I would be remiss if I did not thank the single most important person to me in the writing of this book — my daughter, Meribah Knight. I owe so much to her for bringing to me her profound understanding of ballet and her sensibilities of music and movement. Much of what I have written about the classes and the performances comes from Meribah's own experiences as a young ballerina. Specifically, the scene in the book in which Léontine Beaugrand instructs Sylvie in performing a flawless *tour jeté* was taken almost verbatim from my own daughter's recollection of her ballet teacher, Jacqueline Cronsberg of the New England Ballet Workshop, teaching her this very difficult step. Also, there were Meribah's insights concerning the strength that comes from the core of one's body and how awful it feels when things are not aligned. Her use of the word *floppy* said it all for me. She also described a feeling as if everything is "out of whack." I felt this latter expression would be too modern for my story. The miniature *pas de deux* that Sylvie and Isabel choreographed to fool Sylvie's mother into thinking they had been practicing was actually choreographed by my daughter. I asked her if she could make something a bit like the little swans' variation that she had often danced in *Swan Lake*, but for two instead of four dancers. So she did on our porch in Maine. She taught it to me so I could write it. I write a lot better than I dance. But the memory of learning it from her that summer day I shall always treasure.

Best of all was Meribah's sensual description of the feeling of a dancer doing a center adagio combination in which "from some hidden place" her legs emerge and her arms would float up "like a flower blooming." Finally, there was the unforgettable exuberance she felt when she did a triple pirouette in a class being taught by Kyra Nichols. I was there to see it and after class she came running up to me and said, "Mom, I don't know how it happened. I was coming out of the second rotation and I thought, *I can go around again.* And I did! It was like some other force had taken over my body. Mom, it was so cool!"

Cool was another word I did not think would fit this story. But my daughter is way more than cool. She is a classic. So it is to her that I dedicate this book.

KATHRYN LASKY is the highly acclaimed author of several titles in the Dear America and Royal Diaries lines. She is also the author of the *New York Times* bestselling series Guardians of Ga'Hoole. Kathryn Lasky was awarded the Newbery Honor for the book *Sugaring Time*. She lives in Cambridge, Massachusetts, with her husband.

It's your turn to write a *Portraits* story!

*E*nter the Portraits writing contest—and turn this portrait into a story! Who is the girl in this painting? Where does she live? What is her life like? It's all up to you! In **1500 words or less**, write your very own story about the girl in this portrait. The winning entry will be published in a future Portraits novel.

Entries must be received by December 31, 2005

Young Girl Reading, by Jean-Honoré Fragonard

And be sure to read *Of Flowers and Shadows* Available Now.

Send entries to:
Portraits Writing Contest
557 Broadway
P.O. Box 715
NY, NY 10012

■ SCHOLASTIC

PO